THE SECRËT OF IGUANDO

By the same author:

The Midnight Clowns
Nightland
Rattlesnake and Other Tales (for adults)

THE SECRET OF IGUANDO

ROBERT DODDS

ANDERSEN PRESS · LONDON

For Laura

First published in 2004 by
Andersen Press Limited,
20 Vauxhall Bridge Road, London SWIV 2SA
www.andersenpress.co.uk

British Library Cataloguing in Publication Data available
ISBN 1 84270 327 7

Cover illustration from The Snake Charmer, 1907 (La Charmeuse des Serpents)
by Henri J.F. Rousseau reproduced with permission of the
Musée d'Orsay, Paris, France/Giraudon/Bridgeman Art Library.

Typeset by FiSH Books, London WC1
Printed and bound in Great Britain by Mackays of Chatham Ltd.,
Chatham, Kent

Contents

1
Bandits and Chocolate

Dad came home from work unusually excited.

Claire and Ben were at the kitchen table reluctantly ploughing through their homework. The moment he walked in the door they looked up, glad of the distraction.

It was obvious that something was up. He had a kind of suppressed smirk on his face, and his beard was bristling like a lavatory brush.

'Evening, everyone!' he said, plonking his briefcase in the corner with a flourish.

Mum had already deftly exchanged the magazine she was reading for a tea towel. She liked to look busy. She advanced to peck his cheek and recoiled as if she'd been stung.

'Phew! Elephant!'

'Yes, sorry about that. Minnie has a sore trunk.'

Ben chuckled. 'Remember when she stood on your foot that time!'

This was a vivid and pleasant memory for Ben, but not his father, who winced.

'I certainly do.'

Dad was a zoo vet. Extracting a bad tooth from a crocodile, mending a stork's leg, or attending to an elephant's trunk were all in a day's work for him. Ben was nine, and the envy of all the boys in his class because of his tales of the zoo. According to him, he was frequently allowed into the lions' enclosure, and was on head-patting terms with the cheetah.

Claire, who was nearly thirteen and prided herself on being able to read an adult like an open book, went straight to the point.

'You look pleased with yourself, Dad.'

Mum looked up from her bogus bustling near the cooker and chipped in. 'I was just thinking that as well.'

'What amazing creatures you females are!' Dad grinned. 'I walk in the room. I don't say anything. But you know I'm in a good mood. How do you do that?'

'We just know things,' Claire said, closing her maths book in a way that she hoped suggested a job well done. 'We're better than boys in most ways, actually.'

Ben made a noise like a small motorcycle stalling underwater, to which nobody paid any attention.

'Is it news about the trip, Mike?' Mum asked.

'What trip?' Claire butted in crossly. She didn't like the way Mum and Dad sometimes had secrets.

'Yes, it is,' Dad said, scraping a chair up to the kitchen table. He winked at Claire. 'Didn't know I might be going on a trip, did you?'

'Where to?'

'To Mexico.' He sat down and smirked like a conjuror who has just produced a particularly plump rabbit out of his hat.

'Mexico! What are you going to Mexico for?' Ben said.

2

'Well...there's an expedition to collect new specimens for European zoos. Our zoo has asked me to go. We'll be in a remote area of forests and mountains in the state of Mochaca in Mexico.'

'Motchacker?'

'That's right. Mochaca. My job will be to help select healthy animals, and to look after them, and to sort out details of transporting them safely and humanely back to the European zoos.'

'Wow!' Ben took advantage of the new topic to close his own homework book. 'Cool! Collecting wild animals in the jungle! Will there be tigers?'

'Er – not tigers, no. Not in Mexico. But there might be jaguars.'

Mum came to sit at the table as well, with cups of tea for her and Dad. Tea was always required when important or unusual topics were under discussion.

'So how long is it till you go?' Mum said.

Dad hid behind a big slurp of tea for a few seconds.

'Well, it's not ideal in that respect. It'll be in late July. For three weeks.'

Mum looked as if she'd found a toad in her tea.

'In the school holidays! You're joking!'

Dad wished he was. He spread his hands to show that he was a helpless victim of a cruel fate.

'I know. Believe me, it's not when I would have chosen.' There was a short silence while Mum and Dad sipped tea in the company of their own thoughts.

'Why can't we all go to Mexico?' Claire suddenly said.

'Fantastic idea!' Ben agreed. He didn't know where Mexico was, but he could picture himself riding a mule through a cactus-strewn desert. Wearing a sombrero and capturing rattlesnakes in a sack.

Unfortunately, a chorus of adult problem-finding broke the spell.

'I can't get away from work in July...' Mum was saying.

'It's not a holiday, it's a working trip...' Dad was saying.

'And anyway, think of the cost...' Mum was adding.

'Very expensive...' Dad was agreeing.

And so on.

So that was that. Fun for Dad, but not much fun for anyone else. Claire and Ben shared a look. Cheated again.

'Anyway, you two haven't finished your homework yet, have you?' Mum said.

Later that evening, when Ben and Claire had gone to bed, Alice and Mike Swift were settled in the cosy habitat of the sitting room. Mike was drinking tea, and looking at a library book about Mexico. Alice was drinking red wine, and appeared to be reading a women's magazine. Her thoughts however were focused on the summer holidays, when the children usually spent several mornings a week at the zoo with Mike.

But not if he was in Mexico.

She looked resentfully over the top of her magazine,

4

and saw that her husband had put his fingers and thumbs into a kind of ring shape in front of his face. He was peering at her through the gap. This strange gesture usually preceded the announcement of some crackpot scheme or other.

'Well?' she said.

'You know...' he said slowly, '...I wonder if it would be possible for them to come to Mexico for part of the time – the two weeks after school's broken up.'

'*What?*'

Mike narrowed the gap in his fingers, so that he couldn't see Alice quite so clearly.

'Yes. They could fly out for the last two weeks. I'm sure that would be all right with the rest of the party. I could ring Professor Svensson and talk to him. What an adventure it would be for them! They'd learn so much about life in another country. Broaden their horizons.'

Alice goggled at him. 'I don't believe this! They're just going to make their way to you, are they? In the Mexican jungle somewhere? On their own. Asking the way from locals, that sort of thing?'

'No, no. They could fly out to Mexico City as "unaccompanied minors". It's a direct flight from Heathrow. You'd hand them over to the airline to be looked after, and they'd hand them over to me at the airport at the other end. Then I'd take them to the camp myself.'

Alice sat for a few moments, stunned. Was this the father of her children talking? Hand them over! Fly

5

them halfway around the world on their own? Her babies!

'Over my dead body!' she said, and took a good gulp of wine.

But later, when she was loafing in the bath, another aspect of the situation occurred to her. Two weeks with the house to herself. No one to cook for and clean up after. No whingeing about how boring the holidays were turning out to be. Trips to the cinema and shops with her rarely-seen girl friends. Or even to that salsa club Anna was always going on about. Slovenly afternoons in front of the telly with wine and chocolates...

Later, in her sleep, images of Mexican bandits feeding her children to wild animals alternated with visions of unrestrained salsa dancing, chocolate eating, and shopping. She woke up at dawn, and poked the slumbering body beside her.

'Mike...' she said.

2
Into the Cauldron

Mum was fussing around them at the airport.

'Claire – did you remember to put the Factor 40 sunscreen in the hand luggage like I said?'

'You put it there, Mum. Remember? Wrapped up in four plastic bags in case it leaks.'

'That's right. I did, didn't I? Did I put the anti-snake bite sucker thing in there as well?'

'I don't think so. But there aren't going to be snakes on the plane, are there?'

Their mum looked as if she wasn't too sure.

'I suppose not. But look where you put your feet once you get off at the other end.'

Claire, in spite of the butterflies crashing around in her tummy, felt that she was much calmer than her mother.

'Mum! Stop worrying!'

A young woman in a bizarre yellow and green uniform loomed up out of nowhere. She smiled at them.

'Hello! Are these the children for Mexico City?'

Their mum looked her up and down as if she might be a kidnapper. She babbled a reply.

'Er – yes. These are . . . er . . . they. Them, I mean. This is Ben and this is Claire.'

'Hello!' The air hostess turned the smile on to full power, proudly revealing the kind of teeth rarely seen outside toothpaste commercials. Her words tinkled like ice cubes. 'I'm Susie, and I'm going to be looking after you until you're met at the other end. Are you ready to go?'

Go! Ben suddenly felt as if he were in a lift, dropping down a huge building at great speed and leaving his stomach behind. That little word brought it home to him that he was actually leaving his mum. Up until now, he'd been completely focused on the trip itself. But now his eyes filled up with tears, and he turned quickly to give her a big hug.

''Bye, Mum!' he said. She was hugging him hard in return. He looked up, and her eyes were watery too.

''Bye 'bye, darling! Have a wonderful time!'

Claire felt a pang of unhappiness as well, but she kept a cheerful face as she embraced her mum.

''Bye, Mum! Speak to you on the phone soon!'

The ice maiden air hostess, who had taken a few steps back from this fire of family warmth, now flashed her teeth again as a signal that it was time to move, and marched off at a good pace. They scurried to keep up with her. At the entrance to International Departures they had a moment to look back. Their mum stood in the distance, waving, a tiny forlorn figure with a brave smile. Already they felt very alone.

It was four in the afternoon when the plane began to descend like a huge gliding bird of prey over Mexico

City. Claire had the window seat and marvelled as the snow-covered volcano towering above the city came into view, the afternoon sun burning like red fire on its rim.

'Look, Ben!' She nudged him, and he looked up from his computer game magazine.

'What?'

'That must be the volcano that Dad told us about. Poppo.'

'It had a much longer name than that...Poppo-catta-something.'

'Yes, but he said it was just called "Poppo" for short.'

Ben leaned across her as the volcano slid by below, and he saw a vast sea of mist lapping up against its sides.

'What's all that fog?' he said.

Claire, who could see further ahead, noticed tall buildings poking out of the murk, catching the sunlight on their windows.

'It's pollution. Smog. Remember? Mexico City is the smog capital of the world, Dad said.'

'Oh, right. Gas masks at the ready, then?'

'Mmm...' Claire gazed in awe at the vast smoky landscape unrolling below the plane. Could a single city be so big? It seemed to go on forever in all directions, like a bubbling, steaming soup which had spilt out of its bowl and was going to cover the whole world.

Their stewardess came by to check that their seat-belts were fastened for landing.

'Nearly there!' She gave them the full benefit of her teeth. 'You'll soon be with your dad!'

9

Claire smiled back, and looked again out of the window. It was hard to believe that their own familiar dad was down there, in that cauldron of strangeness.

The Mexico City airport terminal building was a sea of noise and swirling movement. Thousands of people jostled their way backwards and forwards, and around and around. Ben instinctively took hold of Claire's arm. He could imagine himself swept away in this crowd of brown-skinned strangers like a piece of driftwood bobbing in the froth of a deep ocean. Who knew where he might end up!

'Ow! You're pinching!' Claire objected, and he loosened his grip just a fraction.

The stewardess led them to the queue for passport control, and then to the luggage conveyor belt where they waited forever to see their green backpacks appear. Finally they turned up and the children shouldered them and pushed onwards like two tortoises in the wake of their guide.

'This way!' she said brightly for about the hundredth time, waggling an arm in the air to show them where she was heading. 'You'll be met at the airline office, which is along here on the right.'

The airline office had a small seating area around a rather scrawny potted yucca plant. There was no sign of their dad, but when they arrived, a tall slender Mexican woman with long dark hair jumped up from her chair and came forward with a smile.

'You are Ben and Claire? Yes?'

Claire nodded uncertainly. Who was this?

Ben was thinking that the woman looked like a witch, with her long black hair and black clothing. A young and strikingly beautiful witch, but still a witch. Her lips were painted blood red.

'Your father, he could not come. I am Zarina. I have come instead. To take you!'

3
A Coffin and its Contents

'Why couldn't Dad come?' Ben demanded. 'Is something wrong?'

'No, nothing is wrong.'

Zarina's voice was silky and hypnotic. It reminded Claire of one of the big cats at the zoo, purring contentedly over a hunk of raw meat.

'Your father – he was needed at the camp. Me – I had to come to Mexico City anyway, to make the fixing up for permits and other things. My job is to help the expedition.'

The air hostess interrupted.

'I'm afraid I can't release these children into your care, madam, without proper documents. We have very strict rules about unaccompanied minors.'

Zarina fished in a woven shoulder bag. Strange devilish little faces were intermingled in its intricate pattern with pyramids and lines and squares.

'I have what you need, I think. Ah...here.'

She handed over a small dark red passport. The stewardess opened it and read out.

'Michael Swift. Veterinary Surgeon.'

She showed the photograph to the children.

'Is this your dad?'

Claire looked at the bug-eyed lavatory-brush bearded fellow in the picture. She felt relieved.

'Yes, that's Dad's passport.'

'Also...' Zarina was fishing deeper in the bag. As her hand moved about inside it, the devils on the outside seemed to bulge and wink at Ben.

'...here we are.'

Zarina held out a handwritten note. The stewardess took it and read it aloud.

'*Please allow Ben and Claire Swift to accompany the bearer of this note, Miss Zarina Aguila*. It's signed *Mike Swift*.'

She waved the note under the children's noses.

'Is this your father's writing?'

Claire glanced at the paper, which looked as if a spider had crawled across it with a biro strapped to one leg.

'Yes,' she said, nodding.

'Well, that seems to be all right then,' said the stewardess, looking at Claire with rather dull eyes. Claire realised for the first time how tired the stewardess was. Now she seemed anxious to wash her hands of responsibility for the children. Claire looked at Zarina, who smiled, putting the passport back into her bag.

'Okay,' she said. 'We'll come with you.'

The stewardess held out a form to Zarina.

'Just sign this, will you? And I'll keep the letter... thanks. 'Bye 'bye! Have a lovely time in Mexico, you two!'

And she was off. Although she hadn't even bothered to learn their names, Ben felt sorry to see her go. He had felt protected by her, and wasn't sure he'd feel the same way with Zarina. She was looking at him now, quite intently, as if examining some zoological specimen.

'So – you are Mike's boy! Yes, I can see you are looking the same. Your ears, for example.'

Ben put a hand up to one ear. No one else had ever said he'd got his dad's ears. Zarina turned to Claire.

'And you are having his nose, I think.'

Claire tried to picture her father's nose and couldn't.

Zarina smiled again, showing teeth that were beautifully white, but a little pointed. Her dark eyebrows lay like graceful reclining cats on the smooth couch of her forehead, curtained by long, black, shining hair. Half concealed among its strands, tiny silver claws clutching beads of amber dangled from her ears.

'Come this way. I have a car who is waiting for us.'

They embarked from the calm island of the airline office back into the sea of people charging this way and that around the terminal building. Claire and Ben clung tightly to each other's hands – something they wouldn't have dreamed of doing at home.

When they went out through the door of the terminal building, Ben felt a sudden rush of sensations. Warmth flooded over him, and he realised that the inside must have been air-conditioned. Dazzling light made him screw up his eyes. A thousand suns were glinting from car windscreens and the windows of buildings. His ears were assaulted by a great background roar of motor engines and honking car horns while the foreground was a tangle of foreign voices and tinny pulsing music from a nearby flower stall. There was a tang of acid on his tongue, of flowers and petrol in his nose. He felt bewildered, yet excited, as if he were waking from a long grey sleep into a new vivid reality.

'Wow! Look at all these cars!'

A great landscape of gleaming multi-coloured metal lay ahead – the airport car park. They followed Zarina as she picked her way through the lines of cars until they reached a big black four-wheel-drive vehicle.

'Here we are! This is the expedition's vehicle of the Mochaca Zoological Team. Her name is called La Caja.'

'What does that mean in English?' Ben asked.

'Well – that word might mean "the box". But in this case it means "the coffin"!'

Zarina tapped on the darkly-tinted driver's window with a bare knuckle. Most of the others were adorned with silver rings.

'We Mexicans, we like – what you call it? – the black jokes!' She looked sideways at them.

The window slid downwards, and the children were startled to see an incredibly wrinkled old man grinning toothlessly out at them. Claire felt Ben's clutch on her hand tighten in alarm. Was this a living man or a corpse?

'*Hola! Qué tal?*' croaked a voice made of sandpaper and old sticks rubbing together. The old man's misty brown eyes moved, and searched their faces.

'*Me llamo Ramon!*' he added, then put a thin claw out of the window for shaking.

Claire and Ben shook his hand. Ben felt it was like touching a bundle of dry twigs that had come to life.

Zarina looked amused by the children's consternation.

'This is Ramon. He is our driver. For you it is riding on the back seat with another companion!' Zarina swished her long mane back over her shoulders and opened the back door. Who was going to be lurking in there? Ben wondered.

His eyes, dazzled by the sunlight outside, could just make out a flash of red and green in the gloom. It moved towards him along the back seat in a curious sidelong way. He was panic stricken – it looked like some sort of living puppet. Then a voice even more dry and croaking than the driver's said:

'*Buenos días, amigos!*'

It was Claire who first laughed with relief and understanding. It was a parrot! A great big friendly green parrot with a red face and tail feathers, and a huge curving grey beak. He nodded his head up and down at them, and repeated his greeting.

'*Buenos días, amigos!*'

'He's saying "hello",' Zarina explained, reaching into the vehicle and tickling the parrot under his beak. 'Don't be afraid of him, he's very gentle, and he likes children.'

Ben had instinctively backed away a little from the car door, but Claire detached her hand from his and went forward. She was used to the parrots at the zoo at home, and this one didn't look too frightening.

'He's a military macaw. What's his name?' she asked, putting her head into the car.

'Uva Seca,' Zarina replied. 'It means "dried grape" – I think you call it "raisin". We gave to him that name because he loves to eat raisins.'

'Uva seca! Uva seca!' the bird said excitedly, and Zarina gave the children a few raisins each from a little paper bag in the glove compartment.

'Feed him these, and he is becoming friend for life!' she said.

It took a long time to get out of the city. The streets were choked with wild flocks of cars, all honking like geese. The vehicles moved in a series of mad dashes, and their own little old driver kept pace, peering ferociously at the road under the rim of his steering wheel.

By the time they came out into open country, the sun was sinking in the west, and the fields and distant mountains took on a rich smouldering hue, as if an inferno burned just beneath the surface of the landscape.

'How far is it to the camp, Zarina?' Claire asked, leaning forward. Uva Seca, who had been perching half asleep on her lap, made a little protesting caw.

Zarina looked back over her shoulder.

'We will come there tomorrow, in the afternoon.'

'Tomorrow!'

'Yes. It is a far way. We must drive many hundred

miles. Many miles also through jungle. There has been raining, and so a lot of mud and water. Slow to travel.'

'Where are we staying tonight?'

'Tonight we are coming to my mother in the village who is named Tepestloatan. He is my home village. That place is famous in Mexico for its brujos and brujas. Do you know what that is meaning?'

Zarina had turned slightly more in her seat, and was fixing Claire with her dark eyes. Claire shook her head.

Zarina smiled broadly. All her pointed teeth glinted.

'Wizards and witches, you would call them in English. People who know magic.'

Zarina was staring at her. Claire felt that she was being willed to ask a question, a particular question. Zarina's eyebrows arched upwards, waiting. Claire couldn't help speaking.

'Er...are you...do *you*...know magic?'

Zarina laughed, and turned back to face the front again, breaking the spell.

'Perhaps. A little.'

Claire sat back. She wished Mum or Dad was with her. She wasn't comfortable travelling in a coffin with a witch, a talking corpse and a parrot. With a sense of watching an approaching nightmare, she observed the darkness gathering over the strange landscape as they sped along the highway to Mochaca.

4
Village of Darkness

When night had fallen, the journey seemed endless. But drowsiness crept up on the children, and they were both asleep when a jolt of the car woke them to find that they had stopped at last. They were in a small square surrounded by low white buildings. Burning torches flared in brackets on the walls of the house where they had pulled up, casting a flickering eerie light on all of them as they unloaded their bags. A silhouetted figure appeared in the doorway, and its wavering shadow danced out towards them in the torchlight.

'*Hola, Zarina! Hola, Ramon!*'

It was a woman's voice, old but powerful. She stepped aside for them to enter the house. She was much older than Zarina, but also tall, with long hair in which vivid streaks of white zig-zagged like lightning through the predominant strands of jet black. Her face was channelled with deep wrinkles, like sand when the sea has retreated.

'This is my mother. You can call her Marisol – her Spanish name.' Zarina introduced them. Ben and Claire shook her thin hand, and she smiled and nodded at them.

'Do you speak English?' Claire asked, but Marisol

shrugged and looked towards her daughter. Zarina explained.

'Here nobody speaks the English, I'm sorry. Just me. In fact many people here don't talk even the Spanish very much – the local language is called Ixuatal.'

Zarina showed the children into a small room with two beds covered in Mexican blankets with colourful patterns. Ben noticed that his blanket was home to some little devils like those woven into Zarina's bag.

'It's small, but you stay only during one night. Now, my mother prepares the supper. Would you like if I take you for a little walk around the village? Have you too much tiredness?'

In spite of their weariness, Ben and Claire were curious to look around. They went back downstairs, and waited in the main room while Zarina talked briefly with her mother in the kitchen.

'What do you think of Zarina?' Ben whispered to Claire. This was their first moment alone since they had met her.

'I don't know,' Claire whispered back. 'She's been very friendly, but...'

'I think she's scary,' Ben said.

Claire nodded. Just then, Zarina returned from the kitchen.

'This is very lucky,' she said. 'There is a ceremony tonight – a dance for Mother Nacahue, the mother of the gods. Come quick with me – it may have started by now.'

They followed Zarina out into the night. Immediately they could hear the sound of drumming, and, as they hurried along the street with her, a thin reedy fluting noise came to their ears as well. The houses here had no lights in their windows, and the only sources of illumination were flickering torches fastened to the walls. As they walked, they were accompanied by jerky leaping shadows, like great black puppets let out of their boxes for a night of mad dancing.

Zarina turned sharply into a little alleyway which led steeply downhill, and turned to say something to Claire. Ben was following a few steps behind when a sudden movement at a dark window beside him caught his eye. He turned to look, and for a fleeting moment he saw a face in the darkness within the house. It made him stare, for its eyes were like saucers, and instead of a human nose, it seemed to have a curved beak, like a vulture. It whisked out of sight immediately into the black interior, and it must have brushed against something, for there was a little tinkling of bells as it vanished.

Ben stopped, unsure of what he had seen. He felt a shiver running like a mouse with cold feet along his spine. Then he turned to continue along the dark alleyway. Zarina and Claire were nowhere to be seen!

How could that have happened in two seconds? They must be just a few metres ahead in the blackness. He hurried on.

Soon, the alleyway divided. There was a torch fixed on the wall at the junction. On the right was a set of wide cobbled steps going uphill, and on the left was an archway. Water trickled from a pipe down its slimy stones. Where had they gone? The drumming and fluting sound seemed loudest through the archway, so Ben moved gingerly forward.

Something whisked past him with a swishing robe and hurried on ahead. Something with a beak. Ben stopped, breathless with fear. He felt like hiding somewhere, in some safe corner until daylight came. Could he find his way back alone to the house? Or should he go on, hoping that Zarina and Claire were just ahead of him? He decided to go on a little further, carefully, keeping close to the wall. If he didn't find them in a couple of minutes, he'd go back.

The drumming grew louder and louder, and now he could hear voices ahead also. Chanting voices, and a frantic reedy piping sound. The alleyway turned a corner, where firelit puppet shadows wrestled on a blank wall. He peered cautiously around the corner.

It was an open space at the edge of the village. Here there were many torches burning on tall poles, and a bonfire. Beyond was a dark backdrop of rustling trees. Beside the walls of the last houses, the villagers were gathered.

Near to the fire, two lines of strange characters were facing the onlookers and dancing towards them in little hopping steps, like birds. The figures were enveloped from head to toe in curtains of what looked like moss, which flailed around them as they jigged from side to

22

side and up and down. Only their arms protruded – their legs and feet were invisible. They wore wooden masks carved into frightening staring expressions. With wild gestures they shook big round rattles decorated with bright red and yellow feathers.

The figures got nearer and nearer, their movements becoming more frenzied. The monstrous masks loomed closer and closer, their great hollowed-out eyes staring at Ben. Their mouths gaped, bristling with crooked pointed wooden teeth. He felt panic rising and got ready to run. They were almost upon him! Just as he took his first backward step, one of them shouted something which the others repeated, and they all whirled around and started to dance off in the other direction. Ben became aware that he had been holding his breath, and exhaled a long low sigh of relief.

When the dancers reached the bonfire, where the drummers and flute player stood, they stopped. The villagers immediately began chattering to each other excitedly, and some of them were looking inquisitively off to the left. He followed their gaze, and spotted Zarina and Claire. Claire saw him at the same moment, and waved at him to come over.

'I thought you'd got lost!' she said.

Zarina was standing just beyond her, and smiled at Ben. Somehow Ben had the feeling she knew that he'd seen something strange.

Then, out of the darkness, a very old man approached them. He had streaks of green paint on his forehead and his cheeks, and wore a big cape of dark green and red cloth which swished along the ground as he walked. The other villagers drew aside as he reached them, and Zarina bowed towards him. They both made a curious movement of their hands, like birds fluttering down to land, then the old man began speaking to Zarina in the high-pitched Ixuatal language.

'What do you think they're saying?' Ben whispered to Claire. But her attention had been taken by an old woman, who was pointing towards the fire and trying to make her understand something.

Ben watched Zarina and the old man talking. From their glances, it seemed obvious that they were discussing something about the children. Suddenly the old man jumped up in the air with a shriek that made Ben's heart somersault. For a moment his great cloak billowed about him and he seemed to hover just above the ground. His eyes grew round, like an owl's, and the staring black pupils were directed at Ben. It was only a moment, and then he was back on the earth, as if he had just been standing on tiptoe. He bowed curtly to Zarina, glanced at Ben with a frown, and walked off.

'Did you see that?' Ben said shakily to Claire.

'What?' Claire said.

But Zarina interrupted. 'Come on – the ceremony has all finished, and now it is time we are eating.'

5
Brujos

The next day Ben was woken by the sound of a cockerel crowing in the darkness. He lay for a while trying to get back to sleep. He had been dreaming about flying – swooping and gliding over a vast green forest – and he wanted to do it again. But the cockerel was merciless, and eventually he sat up in bed and twitched aside the curtain to look out of the window. In the grey dimness he saw movement in the sky – a flock of birds circling over the village. Big birds, but he couldn't be sure what sort they were. Eagles didn't fly in flocks. He kept watching intently, but before the light was strong enough to identify them, they had vanished. It was a cloudy day that was dawning, dark banks of vapour hanging low over the rooftops. Ben watched as heavy drops of rain began to make dark blobs on the ground below. He heard Claire stretch and yawn behind him. It was time to get up and go in search of Dad!

They set off about an hour later, after breakfasting on soft round tortillas served with fried eggs and a spicy green sauce. Uva Seca perched watchfully on the back of Zarina's chair, and got some titbits of tortilla. They could hear the rain falling heavily while they ate, but it had stopped by the time they were ready to leave. They went to the doorway with their packs, and immediately Ramon drove up in the coffin as if by magic.

'*Buenos días, amigos!*' he cackled, the dry parchment of his skin crinkling into a hideous grin.

The children and Zarina stowed their bags in the back and climbed aboard. Uva Seca hopped onto Claire's lap and shuffled his feet around until he was comfortable, leaning back slightly against her shoulder.

Zarina's mother waved them off, and they twisted and turned through the village's narrow, bumpy streets.

'Look!' Ben said, suddenly, nudging Claire's elbow.

'What?' Claire said.

Ben pointed to a huge tree whose twisted trunk loomed like an arthritic giant over the last house in the village. Steam coiled up from its leaves as the rain evaporated in the growing heat. Standing in the shelter of its enormous green canopy was a group of men swathed in red and green cloaks, their faces streaked with green paint. Their heads turned to follow the car as it drove past, their eyes impassive and unblinking. They looked like great buzzards, standing with their wings folded, and Ben thought uneasily of the flock of large birds he had seen returning to roost as the dawn broke.

'What are those men doing?' he asked.

Zarina turned in her seat.

'Those are some of the brujos that I told you. Magicians.'

'What do they do with their magic?' Claire asked.

'They have powers that come out of the forest. They

can repair those who have sickness and they give advice. They know the secrets of all creatures. They can speak with the voices of animals.'

'Do they always use their powers for good?' Claire asked.

Zarina didn't reply straight away. Then she said, 'Good can mean many things.'

She seemed about to say more, but then fell silent.

Ben felt a little foolish, but asked his question anyway. 'Can they . . . er . . . fly, at all?'

Zarina laughed loudly, and Uva Seca, who was already dozing off, woke and squawked, '*Qué pasa? Qué pasa?*'

Ben thought that the laugh sounded false.

'What has make you think that, Ben?' Zarina said, turning round in her seat to look at him.

'Well, last night, I thought the old man who spoke to you – he was one of the brujos, wasn't he?'

'Yes. The leader of the brujos.'

'Well, I thought he . . . sort of . . . flew a little off the ground when he finished talking to you.'

Zarina smiled.

'I don't think so. It was just a – how do you say – flickering of the torches, perhaps.'

Her eyes were on his own, daring him to challenge her assertion.

'Oh,' he said, lamely.

'How far is it to the camp, Zarina?' Claire asked, breaking the tension that had grown. Zarina shook a strand of hair from her eyes.

'Only about twenty miles. But, like you can see from the road, it will be taking two hours to arrive there.'

The road ahead was like a snake of red mud slithering through the trees. Already, as soon as they left the village behind, the surface had deteriorated into a series of hummocks and potholes, and Ramon was guiding the vehicle between these obstacles with much quiet muttering. In the rear-view mirror they could see his wizened face all bunched up in lines of intense concentration.

Claire looked at the landscape ahead. The trees around them just here were growing quite thinly, but further on the land rose into steep-sided hills covered in thick vegetation. Here and there, great pinnacles of rock lifted angrily out of the canopy to point like giants' fingers at the sky. On the distant horizon, blue jagged mountains stood like bared fangs. As the sun was breaking through the clouds now, and heating up the air, water vapour flowed from the tops of the trees, as if a hundred forest fires were starting. It was a mysterious, exciting, frightening scene, quite unlike anything else she had ever come across.

Meanwhile, Ben was trying to engage Uva Seca in conversation.

'Hello!' he kept saying, but the parrot simply cocked his red and green head to one side, and stuck out his dry little tongue.

'Hello!' Ben said, 'Say "hello!"'

Zarina passed Ben a little bag of raisins.

'Say the word and hold the bag where he is seeing it. He'll know what he's got to do.'

Uva Seca watched the bag intently as Ben took it.

'Hello!' Ben repeated.

Uva Seca made a lunge for the bag, but Ben snatched his hand out of reach.

'Hello!' he said again.

The parrot made a sound like an old man clearing his throat, and then said 'Hello!' perfectly. He looked expectantly towards the bag.

Ben was delighted, and gave him three raisins immediately. While the car slid and lurched onwards, Uva Seca learned 'hello', 'Ben', 'Claire', and 'pieces of eight', and finished all the raisins in the bag.

After what seemed an eternity of bouncing and slithering along, their road was joined by a small river which came rushing out of the forest. In front they could see one of the giant's fingers of rock above the trees.

'The camp, he is quite close now, in a place beside this river,' Zarina said.

Sure enough, a few minutes later they came to a big clearing in the trees. They could see a single blue tent, and four vehicles parked in a line – pick-up trucks loaded with boxes and empty cages.

'I can't wait to see Dad!' Claire said to Ben. 'I can hardly believe he's here, in such a strange hidden-away place.'

'No. Just imagine!' Ben replied, scanning the clearing eagerly. He too felt suddenly excited at seeing Dad. He had his speech all prepared – 'Doctor Livingstone I presume?'

'It's strange,' Zarina said. 'There should be more tents.'

Ramon steered the coffin to a halt, and the children jumped out immediately, looking about them.

But no one came forward to greet them. Ramon tooted the horn, causing Uva Seca to squawk in protest inside the car, and some invisible bird to flap away with a panicky cry in the trees.

'Let's look in the tent!' Ben suggested.

The children ran across the grassy space and unzipped the flap of the tent to look inside. There was nothing there but cardboard boxes filled with tins and packets of food. They came out again and Zarina joined them.

She had a worried frown on her face. Claire thought she looked pale too.

'This is very strange,' she said. 'I wonder to what place are they disappeared.'

6
Missing!

'What's happened, Zarina?' Claire said, trying to stay calm. 'Where's Dad?'

Zarina ran a jewelled hand through her long dark hair. Her eyes were scanning every part of the clearing. Claire couldn't decide whether she looked frightened or guilty.

'I don't know why are they gone. This is where we were all camping. When I going two days ago to collect you from the airport, here was everyone.'

'They couldn't have been attacked – by wild animals?' Ben said.

Zarina shook her head with a wry smile.

'The wild animals would have taken away six tents with them? No. I'm going to look into the cars, to see if they have put any note for us.'

Zarina went from one to another of the parked vehicles, which were splattered with red mud like their own. They were all locked, and no notes were visible either inside or stuck to the windows. The children trailed along disconsolately behind her.

'Well,' Zarina said, after finishing her inspection, 'I think now we have to use our heads to work out where they are gone. They must have gone on foot. There is a donkey, which, maybe, carry the tents. And they can't

31

have been left more than since yesterday in the morning. Let's look for signs about the direction they go.'

'Wouldn't they have gone further along the road?' Ben asked.

'No. The road goes only to an old logging station, a few miles further on, where is nobody. As well, I'm sure if they were going on the road they would have taken the cars. They must have had some reason to move camp. To be coming nearer to something they had found, perhaps.'

'Or to be further away from something,' Ben said. He looked around the empty clearing suspiciously. Who knew what might be lurking just out of sight, in the trees and bushes on its edge?

'Let's take a good search around,' Zarina said.

The three of them started to make a circuit of the clearing, scrutinising the ground and the vegetation. Eventually they found a place where the damp grass was trodden down and trampled and they were able to follow a trail of muddy footprints and broken branches down a short slope to the edge of the river. There were many large stones and boulders in the shallow water, and it was quite easy to cross. On the other side however the ground was firmer, and undergrowth was sparse. No matter how they rooted about, they could find no definite trace of which way the party had gone.

'We can only go back and wait,' Zarina said at last.

'But Dad wouldn't go off deliberately, when he knew we were coming today! There must be something wrong!' Claire said. She felt desperate.

'What other thing can we do but wait?' Zarina said. 'We can't find their trail.'

The sun had completely broken through the morning rain clouds now and was high in the sky. The children found a shady spot under a tree and lay on a blanket that Zarina gave them. They felt despondent and frustrated, and their low spirits – combined with the warm still air – allowed the jet lag of their journey to Mexico to catch up with them. Soon they were drifting in and out of sleep.

Ben didn't know how much later it was, but voices woke him. He listened for a moment with his eyes shut. Zarina was shouting in Ixuatal, her voice high-pitched, like a chainsaw buzzing savagely at a tree trunk. A low bleating response came intermittently, from a voice he didn't know. He opened his eyes and saw on the far side of the clearing that Zarina's words were directed at a man in denim shorts and a grubby white tee-shirt. He had long black hair which fell forward in a fringe partially covering his eyes. A big hooked nose protruded like a parrot's beak from his dark brown face. He kept his head down.

A thin grizzled donkey stood nearby nibbling at the grass. It looked unconcerned by the row going on beside it.

Ben became aware of another presence out of the corner of his eye, and turned. Sitting cross-legged on the ground was a bearded figure, hunched over, scribbling in a notebook. A figure wearing a floppy off-white cotton hat. A familiar, bespectacled figure...

'Dad!' Ben shouted excitedly, sitting up.

Dad looked up from his notebook and his face lit up with a grin of delight.

'Hello, Ben! You were having a lovely sleep, so I didn't want to wake you.'

Ben scrambled up and gave him a huge hug.

'You're sweaty!' he complained, sniffing.

Dad patted his back fondly.

'Ha! Wait and see what you smell like after a few hours' trekking through the jungle!'

Claire stirred, disturbed by their voices. She sat up, blinked blearily, and then relief and happiness flooded into her.

'Dad! You're here! Thank goodness!' She felt like crying with relief, but managed to sniffle back the tears as she embraced him.

'Where were you, Dad?'

'Well, you're going to find out. It's really rather amazing.' Dad had an air of suppressed excitement that betrayed itself by the little lines curling upwards at the edges of his mouth. 'We'll have to set off quite soon, to get there by nightfall.'

'*Where?*'

'Well, it's a place Pierre Rabanade discovered. He's a French naturalist who is one of our party. He disappeared early the day before yesterday with Juan – that's the man over there who's getting a hard time from

34

Zarina. They came back just as it got dark, and Pierre was terribly excited. Apparently he'd found a lake with a new kind of frog living at its margins – a totally new, undiscovered frog. What about that!'

Ben and Claire tried to look suitably impressed.

'The lakeside was ideal for a new camp, he said, and the area around it looked interesting. He saw all sorts of animal tracks and it seemed a good idea to move our base camp over there. So yesterday we did that, and this morning I came back with Juan to collect more food supplies and meet you. It just took a bit longer to get here than we expected.'

'We were scared,' Claire admonished him.

'I thought you'd been eaten!' Ben said.

Dad put his arms around their shoulders. 'I'm sorry you got a fright. But here we all are, safe and sound!'

'Why's Zarina so angry with that man?' Ben asked.

Dad glanced over at the scene at the other side of the clearing.

'I don't really know. I suppose because we didn't get back here by the time you arrived.'

Claire snuggled in close to his side and looked over again towards Zarina. She had finished shouting at the man, and now stood with her arms folded, staring into space. She looked like a black thunder cloud from which lightning might flash at any moment. Claire thought that Dad's explanation couldn't be right. Zarina was very, very angry – but why?

7
Down the Funnel

It was about half an hour past midday when the party was ready to set off for the new camp. The donkey was called Mariposa, which Zarina said meant 'butterfly' in Spanish. Patting the grey creature's bony head, Claire had to wonder who had dreamed up such an unsuitable name.

By the time Mariposa was loaded up with boxes of tinned and dried food, and some collapsible cages, it would have been hard to say who looked more fed up – the donkey or her master Juan, who poked her halfheartedly with a sharp stick in the flanks to make her move. Zarina spoke curtly to him from time to time, and he kept his eyes well hidden behind his fringe of black hair.

'What's Juan done to upset you?' Dad said once, but Zarina just shook her head and said nothing.

Ramon had driven off, back to Tepestloatan, but Uva Seca, to the children's delight, was travelling with them. He perched on top of the boxes on Mariposa's back, peering ahead like the captain of a ship standing on deck in stormy seas. Whenever the donkey stumbled and jolted him, he clucked loudly and disapprovingly.

They crossed the stream and at first made swift progress through gently rising woodland. There was little undergrowth, and their feet rustled in the thick layer of brittle leaves that had gathered on the ground. Soon however, they were panting as the slope grew steeper and steeper, and the trees fell away. Their route wound in and out of huge rounded boulders that seemed to have been scattered about in some giants' game of marbles.

Eventually, after several hours, they reached the rim of a steep rocky ridge and found themselves gazing down into a vast bowl of forest which was surrounded on all sides by jagged mountains. The sun was low to their left, and already the shadows of the mountains were creeping like a tide of dark water across the landscape below them. Ben stared in wonder. There was something different about this unexpected place. Nothing he could put words to. But it gave off a kind of feeling of *aliveness*. Looking down at the green canopy, he thought it was like the surface of a deep ocean, hiding who knew what mysterious creatures swimming below. And, like green waves, the trees seemed to ripple this way and that, pulled by deep currents. Even the air above the great bowl shimmered strangely, as if vast invisible shapes moved through its substance.

Juan lifted the fringe of hair from his eyes and pointed with his donkey prodder. He spoke in Spanish, perhaps thinking the children would understand.

'*Acá! Al lado del lago!*'

Zarina pointed out a glint of water to the children.

'There is a lake. They are camped beside it.'

Ben shielded his eyes and studied the scene.

'That looks like it's miles away!'

'No. Only another hour and a half. But we must hurry to get there in front of the dark.'

Claire scanned the ridge to either side of them. Ahead, the ground shelved steeply downwards, ending in what looked like a precipice.

'How do we get down?' she said to Dad.

'Wait and see!' He winked at her. Dad could be very irritating sometimes.

Juan led the way to a clutch of big boulders along the ridge. The boulders leaned inwards conspiratorially, hiding whatever was in their midst. Juan circled around with Mariposa to the far side. There, and only there, was a gap wide enough for the donkey to squeeze through. Ben was the next in line, and was quite unprepared for what was concealed within the huddle of stones.

'We're not going in there, are we?' he asked Dad, who squeezed through the gap just behind him.

'That's right. Amazing that Pierre Rabanade found this at all, isn't it!'

Ben saw Zarina scowling for some reason. Perhaps she had grazed herself on the rocks.

It was a kind of funnel going down into the ground. Not quite a cave, for daylight filtered in through fissures in the surface above. It was filled with fallen rocks, which made a kind of staircase. Ben peered down into the gloom. The funnel twisted after about forty metres. There was a strange sound coming from down below, a sort of low roaring noise. He didn't like it.

But Juan was already urging the reluctant Mariposa down into the hole. Uva Seca squawked in protest and shifted his claws to get a better grip on the packing case that he was riding on. Zarina said something soothing to him.

As they picked their way downwards, the gloom grew darker, and the roaring sound grew louder.

Suddenly, Claire screamed. Something had brushed through her hair! Dad cried out, 'Look out!' and she shielded her face as a great cloud of small black flapping dishcloths came hurtling up the tunnel towards them.

'Bats!' she heard Ben exclaim beside her. The little creatures flooded past, making a noise with their wings which was like hundreds of people applauding, but with gloves on. Then they were gone, as suddenly as they had come. Dad looked after them.

'They must fly out of here at dusk every night,' he commented.

'They gave me a fright!' Claire said.

'Me too, actually!' Dad admitted, taking off his floppy cotton hat and mopping his brow with a handkerchief. 'Anyway, night falls quickly in the tropics, so we must hurry if we're to get to the camp before darkness!'

They pressed on with a new sense of urgency. It was difficult, as the rocky funnel was steep, and some of the stones moved as you put your weight on them.

At last the craggy roof above them opened out, and they found themselves in a narrow gorge. Soon it grew wider, and the ground became more level. They could see forest ahead of them.

'Are we at the bottom of those cliffs now?' Claire asked Dad.

'Yes. We're down at the level of the lake now. Another hour or so from here – as long as we don't get lost.'

Ben cocked an ear. Without his noticing, the roaring noise had vanished.

'What was that sort of booming noise we could hear in the rocks?' he asked.

Zarina overheard, and answered his question.

'There is a big waterfall near here. The sound of the water is coming through the caves in the cliffs.'

Dad looked surprised.

'You didn't say you'd been here before, Zarina.'

'Once. A long time ago,' she replied, and then strode forward quickly before he could say anything else.

The light was almost gone when the weary party stumbled into the camp. On the strand beside the lake, a bonfire was crackling and throwing out a cheerful glow, and figures were seated around it on logs. A row of tents was pitched beneath the looming green wall of the surrounding forest. And every step of the way, in spite of his tiredness, Ben had felt that they were being watched by a million invisible eyes.

8
A Meal of Bank Notes

At the fireside a white-bearded figure leapt up like a kangaroo at their approach and came forward to shake the children's hands with a vigorous horizontal pumping action, as if inflating bicycle tyres. His eyes twinkled in the firelight. Ben thought he looked the very picture of an eccentric explorer from comics and films, all wild matted hair and baggy shorts with bulging pockets and peculiar stains.

'So gratified to encounter you! Attach no significance to your father. He *will* denominate me as "Professor Svensson", but you must give me the appellation "Henry"! That way, he will get into the habit as well!'

Professor Svensson's English was heavily accented, and Ben assumed that some of the words he didn't understand must be Swedish or Polish or something. Claire thought that Professor Svensson might have learned his English from the *Oxford English Dictionary*, not from actually speaking to English people.

Their dad laughed.

'Well, since I've known you for years through your books as "Professor Svensson", the world's leading authority on central American wildlife' (here the Professor shook a hand to wave away the praise like a

41

bothersome fly) 'I keep forgetting that you're just plain "Henry" now!'

'Nonsense! Nonsense!'

The Professor subsided back to his log with a wink at the children. Next they were introduced to a long thin Frenchman with a moustache lurking like a furry caterpillar on his top lip. His eyes were heavily lidded, and he blew smoke from his cigarette down his nose as he remained seated and greeted them with a lift of one eyebrow and a sort of twitch of his mouth.

'This is Pierre Rabanade, our lizard and snake expert.'

Claire was not surprised. There was something snake-like about Pierre Rabanade.

The third member of the group was, by contrast, up on her feet and beaming at the children and their father. She was quite small, pretty, with spiky blonde hair, a nose ring, multiple earrings, and bright red lipstick. She would be in her twenties, and Claire thought she looked ready for a night on the town.

'Anneka works at the Amsterdam Zoo,' Dad explained. 'An expert on tropical birds, among other things.'

'Gerraway!' Anneka exclaimed in a broad Yorkshire accent. She looked embarrassed. 'I'm just a beginner! Don't pay any attention to this expert malarky, you two!'

Dad shrugged and smiled. 'It's true, nevertheless. Anyway – that just leaves our other porter and the cook – they're over there preparing supper.'

Dad led them to where two men sat cross-legged on

the ground beside a low camping table, cutting vegetables with curving villainous knives.

'This is Trueno, our cook, and Juan's brother José, our second porter.'

The two men looked up at the children. Trueno flashed his teeth and waved his knife at them in a way that seemed half friendly, half threatening. His belly spilled over the waistband of his trousers and rested like a small whale on his crossed legs, and Ben wondered how he had squeezed through the rocks at the entrance to the funnel. José's eyes stayed hidden behind a fringe of hair identical to his brother's. He too had a nose like a parrot's beak. It occurred to Claire that a miniature nodding version of José or Juan would have made a good novelty ornament for the back shelf of someone's car.

'Are the porters twins, Dad?' she said, as they went back to the bonfire.

'Yes. I can't tell them apart.'

'I thought the expedition would be much bigger,' Claire went on. 'I thought there'd be dozens of people.'

'Well, it's best not to have a crowd. It only disturbs the animals. Anyway – let's get you organised in your tent before supper's ready.'

They collected their backpacks, which had been carried by Mariposa, and went with Dad to the line of tents. Dad shone his torch into one of them.

'This one's yours – in between mine and Anneka's. Professor Svensson is next to me on the other side, unfortunately.'

'Why unfortunately?'

Dad whispered, as if telling an important secret. 'He snores like a wart hog!'

They all giggled.

'Which reminds me,' Dad went on, 'how's Mum?'

'She's fine. She sends her love.'

'Good. I expect she'll be missing us all. Probably having a lot of quiet evenings at home with a good book. Now, let's get you sorted out.'

'Dad...' Ben said, as they unrolled their sleeping bags, 'did Pierre... what was his name?'

'Rabanade.'

'Did he find this place on his own?'

'Well – my theory is that either Juan or José must have shown him. One of them went with him when he was exploring.'

'It is sort of hidden away, isn't it? I mean, I wonder if there's any other way in or out, apart from down through that cave thing.'

'It certainly looks as if it's cut off by mountains on all sides, as far as you can see from the top of the ridge, coming in.'

'Did you see the special frogs?' Claire asked.

'Not yet. We spent the whole day yesterday just getting here and setting up camp. But Pierre was certain that this was a brand new type of frog. What Professor Svensson...'

'*Henry!*' Ben and Claire chorused.

'... sorry, Henry hopes is that because this area is

isolated from the outside world, and undisturbed by humans, we may find other unique creatures.'

'Wow! Like in *The Lost World*!' Claire said.

'Yes – sort of. Although we're not expecting dinosaurs.'

'Who knows? Has this area been explored before?'

'Well, we don't think zoologists have ever been here before. Zarina says not. And the only village anywhere near here is Tepestloatan, where you stopped last night.'

'So what's it called, this place?' Ben asked.

'None of us is sure. Zarina said today that it hadn't got a name. What I do know is that Trueno . . .'

'The cook?'

'Yes. He seemed terribly reluctant to come here. He was shaking his head and complaining all the way to Juan and José. Of course I didn't know what they were all saying, but I kept hearing a word like *Iguando*, so perhaps that's what this place is called.'

They had finished setting things out in their tent. Their torches and water bottles were placed within reach, and the rucksacks stashed at the far end, beyond their lightweight sleeping bags.

They zipped up the mosquito netting flap and went and sat down on a log with the others for supper. Ben felt so tired that it was as if great bags of sand had been tied to his limbs. He could hardly raise his hand to eat the tortillas and fried chicken and vegetables that Trueno served them on plastic plates. Later, he was vaguely aware of his dad carrying him off to the tent, and Claire crawling in beside him. The last thing he knew was the sounds of the jungle outside, a mixture of rustlings and hootings and screeches, merging in his dreams with the voice of Uva Seca crying, '*Beware of Iguando! Beware of Iguando!*'

Claire also was just drifting off to sleep when low voices disturbed her. She thought she could hear Zarina, speaking quietly but angrily. She looked out through the fine mesh of the mosquito flap, and made out the dark shapes of Zarina with Juan and José silhouetted against the fire, which had burned low, but still gave out a fitful orange light. Everyone else must have retired to their tents.

There was something strange going on. Zarina was standing over the twins, who seemed to be either kneeling or crouching. They shook their heads and moaned quietly. Zarina was handing something to them, which they were putting in their mouths. But it didn't look like food. It looked like slips of paper.

Claire stared astonished at the scene. There was no doubt about it – the twins were actually eating these slips of paper! And not enjoying it, that was certain. Then a part of the puzzle, only a part, fell into her understanding. It was money! Zarina was making them eat money. But what was the sense in that? And why should they obey Zarina anyway?

Claire withdrew her eyes from the disturbing sight and got back into her sleeping bag. She lay there revolving the mystery around and around in her mind until she found that she was being pushed along in a wheelbarrow by Zarina in a parade of flying donkeys, walking boulders, and money-eating bats. The parade filed into a deep cave, where she fell sound asleep.

9
The Speaking Forest

The next morning Ben and Claire got up just in time to see Juan, José and Mariposa leaving the camp. Their dad, washing his beard in a small plastic bowl outside his tent door, explained why.

'The Professor has sent them back to base camp to get more boxes and cages. Let's hope we find animals to fill them!'

They joined the others beside the still glowing embers of last night's fire, where they were drinking coffee and discussing the day's plans. Trueno brought some toast and plates.

'I will cover the area *au bord du lac* to the north,' said Pierre, wreathed in smoke from his first cigarette of the day. 'That is where the yellow-spotted frogs were.'

'I will accompany you, if I may, Pierre,' said Professor Svensson, splashing his coffee about in his excitement. No wonder his clothes were all stained, Claire thought. 'If indeed you have found a new member of the family Ranidae, this will be a splendid day for science!'

'Perhaps it would be better if I am on my own. It would be less disturbing for the frogs.'

'Not at all! I insist!'

The Frenchman's eyelids lowered a fraction and he blew out a sharp puff of smoke, like a kettle letting off steam.

'Very well, if you must.'

Professor Svensson turned to Anneka, who was feeding bits of banana to Uva Seca. The parrot seemed to have taken a bit of a shine to her, and cawed 'Anneka' softly between beakfuls.

'What about you, Anneka? Upon what course of action will you embark?'

Anneka pulled thoughtfully at her nose ring.

'Well, Henry, I was listening out last night, right? And there were lots of things you might expect to hear. For instance, there was a *tsip-tsip-tsip-tsip-wheeeeoooo*!'

She threw her head back to emit this strange sound, and everyone looked startled, especially Uva Seca, who backed away slightly along the log he was standing on.

'Ah – a double-toothed kite?' Professor Svensson said.

'Spot on!' said Anneka, impressed.

'Your impersonation is so accurate!' the Professor said, with a smug little smile nonetheless that he had guessed correctly.

'Then there was a *peter-peter-peter-peter*!'

'Green Shrike-Vireo,' the Professor nodded.

Anneka grinned. 'And a *yoik-yoik-yoik-yoik*!'

This was a noisy raucous sound, and Uva Seca's feathers bristled. He cocked a suspicious eye at Anneka.

'Yellow-cheeked parrot?' the Professor queried.

49

'Spot on again, Henry! You certainly know your bird calls!'

'Wow! Can you teach me some of those?' Ben said. 'Yoik! Yoik!!'

'You sound like a pig with a stick up its bottom,' Claire said disdainfully.

'Claire!' Dad tut-tutted.

Anneka smiled at Ben. 'I can teach you some if you like. Any road, Henry, I heard some other cries that I'd never heard before, so I'll go into the forest just away from the lake and see what I can spot with my binocs.'

'Excellent. And what will you do, Mike?' said Professor Svensson. 'Will you and your progeny associate with us along the lake edge?'

Pierre Rabanade, who had been haughtily ignoring the bird-calling, now made a snake-like writhing motion with his neck.

'No! I must really protest, Professor, for the sake of my frogs! We must proceed quietly, not like a herd of elephants.'

He looked at Ben and Claire as if he could see trunks and tusks.

Their dad stepped in.

'Don't worry, don't worry. We'll go into the forest with Anneka – is that all right, Anneka?'

Anneka beamed at him. 'Aye. Brilliant!'

Professor Svensson turned to Zarina, who was sitting a little apart, wrapped in a gloomy silence.

'That just leaves you, Zarina. What will you do?'

Zarina stared into the forest, like a cat looking for birds.

'I will look around on my own, Professor. Is that all right?'

'Of course – as you wish.'

He glanced at his watch.

'Everyone has their walkie-talkies, yes? And their whistles, flares, medical kits, yes?'

Everyone nodded.

'Good. Then we rendezvous again here tonight by five o'clock. Or earlier of course if there is excessive precipitation.'

He waved to Trueno, the cook, who shambled over from his camping table with a pile of little packages wrapped in foil.

'Lunch,' their dad explained to Ben and Claire, and they tucked the packages into their small day sacks. Ben's eyes were shining with excitement. This was real adventure! Exploring unknown jungle with Dad, looking for strange beasts. He wished his classmates could see him now!

The forest was eerily silent at first. Dad led the way, glancing at his compass from time to time to steer a course to the east. Claire followed just behind with Anneka, who was friendly and talkative, and wanted to know all about what music Claire liked, and where she went shopping, and who her friends were.

Ben brought up the rear. He let his imagination

improve on the situation. In his fancy, there were fierce man-eating tigers lurking in this jungle, and it was his job to protect his unwary companions by keeping a good lookout. He had quietly picked up a perfect stick to use as a rifle, and already dispatched a couple of the cunning brutes who had tried to sneak up behind him. He felt a little guilty about this game in present zoological company, and stayed far enough away from the others for them not to hear his pretended gunshots.

Gradually though, he lost interest in his fantasy and became increasingly aware of a sort of watchfulness in the forest around him. It was as if the trees, the leaves, the trailing rope-like lianas, even the humps and hollows on the ground, were all looking at him. Pale brown termite mounds were dotted about, two metres high. They were like people, temporarily frozen into statues, and only waiting for him to turn his back before coming back to life. Some of them had holes like ragged mouths, calling out a silent warning. He started to see faces everywhere. On the trees, beak-like noses emerged from the twisted trunks, and swivelling eyes appeared to watch him pass. The canopy far above rustled in a breeze which you couldn't feel down below, and it was as if millions of tiny shivery little voices were crying out.

As Ben walked on, the tension was like a taut wire stretching tighter and tighter around his chest. He felt that the whole forest was speaking to him, trying to tell him something important, but he just couldn't understand its words.

10
A Shock among the Rocks!

After a while, they came to a place where the trees thinned out and gave way to a rising slope covered in long wispy grass. At the top were some big rocks.

'Why don't we set up a hide in them rocks for an hour or two?' Anneka suggested. 'It's a good vantage point, and we'll see nowt while we're clattering around ourselves.'

'Good idea,' Dad agreed, mopping his brow with a handkerchief. 'I could do with a sit down anyway.'

They clambered up the slope and found a perfect viewing point between some big boulders. However, it was hot out in the open, so they returned to the edge of the forest to gather long sticks. Dad was in full scout-master mode. He used his Swiss army knife to sever clumps of long grass from the hillside. Under his direction they wedged the sticks between the rocks and used twine (brought smugly forth from Dad's rucksack) to bind the bunches of grass onto the sticks and make a roof.

'Hey up! This is great, isn't it?' Anneka grinned at Ben and Claire. 'Just like building a den, eh?'

When they'd created enough shade, everyone settled down in the makeshift little house and drank deeply from their metal water canteens.

Both Dad and Anneka had binoculars. Anneka offered hers to Ben.

'Do you want first go?' she said.

'Thanks.'

He scanned the open grassland below and the edge of the forest beyond. Almost immediately, he picked up a flash of motion in the tree branches.

'Dad! Monkeys! Down in the trees!'

Dad trained his own binoculars in the same direction.

'Yes! They're red-backed squirrel monkeys. Seven or eight of them. What are they up to?'

Ben studied them. They were eating fruit. But not in the messy squabbling way that the zoo monkeys he was familiar with ate their food. Instead, one of them, sitting on a broad branch, had collected a little pile, and was distributing pieces to the others, who lined up as if at a bus stop.

'That's amazing!' Dad said. 'I've never seen that before!' He scribbled feverishly in his notebook, and after a while, the monkeys moved on.

Ten minutes later it was Claire's turn to spot something. A giant anteater emerged from the gloom beneath the trees into the sunlight and lifted its long pointed snout to sniff the air.

'Dad! Giant anteater!'

Dad swung his binoculars onto the subject.

'Yes. I think he's interested in that termite mound.'

Sure enough, the big creature walked along on its knuckles to a termite mound on the grassy slope in front of them. It got up on its back legs and started bashing at the top of the mound with its claws, like a boxer. Then it shoved its long nose deep into the ruins, and Claire could just see its extended tongue flickering in and out as it feasted on the doomed insects. She lowered her binoculars and looked up at the sky, trying to imagine what a giant anteater would look like if you were the size of a termite.

A whole hour passed by without any more animals being seen. Anneka identified a few bird calls. They ate their packed lunches and a fly buzzed drowsily around their crumbs. After a few more minutes there was a loud snoring sound. Anneka smiled at the children.

'Looks like your dad is having his siesta!'

'Snoring like a hog,' Ben agreed. He was feeling fidgety and bored. He looked at Claire, whose eyelids were heavy.

'Claire!' he said. 'Do you want to come and have a look to see what's beyond these rocks?'

'Sure.'

'Better stay within earshot,' Anneka advised.

'We will.'

They crept quietly out of the hide. If Dad woke up he might not let them go. They scrambled up to the top of a boulder a few metres higher up the hill.

From here, they could see down the other side of the hill. It was a jumble of big sandy brown and reddish rocks, like a child's tower of bricks that has been knocked down in a tantrum. At the bottom of the slope, the forest resumed, marching away until its green leaves turned pale blue and merged in a nebulous haze with the jagged mountains rising far to the east. Huge white clouds were piled up above the mountains, towering shapes of dragons, castles, and full-sailed galleons.

'Let's play hide-and-seek!' Ben said. The rocks were huge, with gaps between them which were ideal for squeezing through.

'Okay then,' Claire agreed.

'Bagsy I hide first!' Ben said. 'Count to fifty!'

Ben loved hide-and-seek. He knew it didn't really matter if you were caught, but it was great fun pretending that some monster was on your trail. He wound his way hither and thither among the rocks with a pleasant sense of panic until he found himself in a nice secret little hollow. He hunkered down and waited, listening for any sound that betrayed his sister's approach.

But as he waited, that sense of being watched that had haunted him earlier returned. His skin prickled, and he found his gaze being drawn off to one side. At first he couldn't make out anything unusual. Then an eye blinked at him from the middle of a rock. A rock with eyes! He froze in terror. But then a part of the rock moved a little bit, and he realised that he was looking at a huge lizard – maybe two metres long – lying out in the sun.

Ben wasn't afraid of lizards as a general rule. But this one unnerved him. It was the same colour as the rock it lay on – a sort of reddish-brown. Was it a chameleon? Or an iguana? It did look very much like an iguana, with a raised ridge running along its back and a kind of flap hanging like a beard below its jaw. But in size it was more like a crocodile.

Its eye continued to watch him beadily. Then, with an utterly unexpected upward thrust of its squat legs, it launched itself off the rock and landed right in front of him!

Ben yelped with fright and scrambled away like a demented spider over the rocks, up the hill towards the others. He didn't look back to see if the lizard was following him. He imagined it hopping along behind him like a kangaroo, getting ready to leap on his back. There was a call in front of him.

'Ben! Where are you?'

Ben emerged from the jumble of rocks to see Claire standing on the big boulder at the top, shading her eyes from the sun.

'Ah! There you are! I looked all over for you.' Then she registered his pale face and wild expression. 'What's happened?'

'A...lizard!' Ben gasped out, leaning against the boulder and catching his breath. He looked back down the hill.

'A lizard? What's the big panic about a lizard?'

'It was...a...big...lizard!'

'How big?'

'Like...a crocodile! But shaped like an iguana!'

'Are you sure?'

'Of course I'm sure. It chased me!'

'A lizard! Chasing people! That's not very likely.'

'It did! Or, at least, it jumped at me.'

Claire looked hard at him, then shrugged. 'Come on. Dad's stirring. You can tell him about it.'

Emboldened by having the others with him, Ben led the way back down the hill to where the lizard had been, but there was no sign of it now. Dad nodded when he said how big it had been, but he said he'd note it down for now in his book just as a 'large iguana'.

On the way back towards the lake, Ben felt more strongly than ever that they were being followed, but no matter how often he whirled around to look, there was never anything to see.

Their group was the first to arrive back at the camp that evening. Trueno had got a barbecue going. He had rigged up a long skewer on two sticks over a bed of burning embers. Mariposa the donkey was tethered nearby, beside a pile of newly brought cages and boxes. Juan and José were watching the food preparations anonymously from under their curtains of hair.

Dad wandered over to the barbecue and said a word or two to Trueno in halting Spanish. Then he seemed to be intrigued by the carcass on the skewer. He stared at it intently, then went over to the mess of skin and bones where Trueno had gutted the animal. He poked about, looking increasingly astonished. Claire and Ben

58

exchanged a look. It wasn't a pretty sight, seeing your own father rooting about in a dead animal's innards. He waved Anneka over with bloody fingers.

Anneka also started rooting about.

'It's disgusting!' Claire said. 'What are they so interested in?'

Finally, Anneka and their dad stopped. Trueno seemed to think that the meat was now cooked to perfection, and he was cutting chunks off onto a plate, burning his fingers in the process.

'What is it, Dad?' Ben said, going over. 'What's so interesting about this stuff?' He pointed at the horrid remains.

'What's so interesting,' Dad replied slowly, 'is that neither Anneka nor I have ever seen an animal like this before. We think it may be a new species.'

Anneka glanced over to Trueno, who was popping a piece of meat into his mouth.

'And now we're having it for supper,' she added.

11
A Meeting by Moonlight

Professor Svensson and Pierre Rabanade had all the bones and bits of fur neatly laid out on Trueno's cooking table. It was like a jigsaw, with the main bit missing. Reluctantly it had been agreed that there was nothing to be done with the roasted meat but to eat it, and Ben found it very tasty indeed, a bit like lamb. Trueno seemed unabashed by his mistake, and had prepared a delicious sauce with herbs to accompany the meat.

But the others ate with the glum expressions to be expected from zoologists chewing on what could possibly be the last remaining specimen of a hitherto undiscovered species. Professor Svensson added salt to his portion with a particularly melancholy air.

'Trueno says there were probably others, Professor,' Anneka said, trying to cheer him up. She spoke enough Spanish to have gathered this view from their cook. 'He says there are bound to be more of them, in the forest.'

'It is a pity we engaged such a trigger-happy fellow in the first place!' said Pierre Rabanade, nibbling daintily on a rib.

'I have confiscated the firearm,' said Professor Svensson. 'I would never have permitted it, if I had known.'

Pierre Rabanade shrugged his shoulders. 'There is some saying I think about the stable doors and the horse bolting?'

The day had been a great success for the reptilian Frenchman. Professor Svensson had been able to verify that the yellow-spotted frogs in the margins of the lake were indeed new to science, and could therefore be called Rabanade Frogs. They seemed to be plentiful, and they planned to capture a few when the expedition was ready to return to base.

After they had all finished eating, Professor Svensson stood up to address them. Darkness had now fallen, and the flames of the campfire illuminated him from below, like a friendly bearded devil.

'Well, today we have had an interesting day, yes? We have found a new frog, the Rabanade Frog.' Here he bowed stiffly towards the Frenchman, who held up a hand to wave away imaginary applause. 'We have seen some innovatory behaviours among red-backed squirrel monkeys, and now we have devoured an unknown dog-sized mammal of the family Canidae. This is, by any standards, an extraordinary day for zoological science, yes?'

Everyone nodded. He took off his spectacles and polished them with a filthy looking handkerchief.

'Good. Now, we have a good supply of boxes and cages conveyed to us, so we are ready to begin collecting specimens. Tonight we will have a night watch at the brink of the lake, where animals may come to drink. The porters have constructed a hide for us, and now that we have consumed sustenance perhaps we should decide who is going to watch first?'

'Perhaps it would be helpful also to make plans for tomorrow?' Pierre Rabanade said, lighting up a cigarette and blowing smoke all over Claire.

As the discussion rolled on, Claire decided she would get up to stretch her legs and look at the moon rising over the lake's surface. She wandered along the beach about two hundred metres or so. Glancing back, the figures around the campfire looked like little toy people and their talk and laughter was a tiny sound in the distance. She shivered in the cool breeze that came across the lake. Moving forward again, she saw a figure standing silhouetted against the silvery surface of the water. A tall figure, with long hair. It was Zarina, standing looking up into the sky over the lake. Claire recalled that she hadn't seen her since the morning. She stopped and glanced back at the campfire, wondering whether to return, or to keep walking forward and speak to Zarina, who was about thirty metres away.

Suddenly, out of the dark sky over the lake came a whooshing, feathery beating noise. 'Wumph! Wumph! Wumph!' Claire hunkered down instinctively amongst a clump of reeds at the water's edge. Something big was out there. Something bigger than a bird. It hovered, flapping, over the water and then came gently down to land near Zarina. The creature's silhouette against the moonlit lake was unrecognisable. What looked like giant wings folded themselves inwards. There was a sort of shaking movement, and a sort of blurred shuddering, and then, to Claire's astonishment, she recognised the outline of the old brujo from the village. In a hissing, urgent voice the brujo began speaking in the strange high-pitched Ixuatal tongue. He seemed to be angry, for he waved his arms violently, and his nose and jaw kept jutting forward like the beak of a vulture. Zarina was shaking her head and trying to calm him down with gentle answers.

Claire herself stayed stock still, terrified that the loud beating of her heart would give her away. Once, Zarina and the brujo stopped speaking and looked towards the campfire, and Claire could only be thankful for her earlier impulse to hide in the reeds.

The brujo and Zarina talked on and on, the one fierce and vociferous, the other pleading and soothing. Finally the brujo swept his cloak up into the air with his arms, and again there was the blurred shuddery movement. He became an indistinct huge looming shadow, then with a sound something between a shout and a squawk, he took to the sky and was gone in an instant, flapping off over the trees of the forest.

Zarina stood for a few moments. She was talking to herself. Perhaps chanting something. Then she started walking back towards the campfire. Claire stayed down in the reeds, curling herself up like a hedgehog into a small invisible ball. With enormous relief, she heard Zarina's footsteps pass by a few metres away on the shingly shore.

Claire felt as if a hole had been cut in the fabric of the normal world, and she had peeped through into a dark and terrible place which lurked unseen behind it. It was like being a small child again, when monsters could be waiting to pounce in any dark corner of the bedroom at night.

She watched until she could see Zarina's dark figure against the glow of the bonfire, as she sat down again with the others. She heard Uva Seca's dry croaking welcome. Then, on unsteady legs, Claire circled around, and came back to the group from the direction of the tents, so that Zarina would not realise where she'd been.

It was very hard to know what to do with her strange knowledge. Only Ben might believe what she'd seen. She felt desperate to tell him about it, and hurried towards the bonfire. She would get him away on some excuse. But when she got there, Ben was gone. And so were Dad and Anneka.

12
Lizards

Ben had grown bored with the adults' discussion, and decided to go and see where Claire was. He thought she'd probably headed towards the tents, on the edge of the forest. He made his way there, shining his pocket torch ahead of his feet. Claire wasn't in their tent, but he was just withdrawing his head from the flap after looking in when he heard a sound behind him.

'Claire?' he said, turning. But where Claire's figure would have been silhouetted against the moonlit water of the lake, there was nothing. He scanned his torch and it picked out glittering eyes. Low down, at waist height. Lizard eyes! A scaly head regarded him steadily, and he heard a kind of hiss like a tyre deflating. It looked like the gigantic iguana-like lizard had tracked him down!

Ben tried to call out towards the campfire, but his throat was as dry as sandpaper and hardly a squeak came out. The lizard took a heavy step towards him, and instinctively Ben turned tail and stumbled back towards the trees behind the tents. He couldn't get rid of the crazy thought that the lizard had sought him out. Once he had got a few metres into the trees, he turned and shone the torch backwards again. For a moment there was nothing to be seen, but then he picked out the big lizard lumbering steadily towards him, its eyes fixed hypnotically on his own. There was such a look of intelligence in its face that Ben spoke to it.

'What is it? Why are you following me?'

But the lizard didn't react to his voice. It just kept coming towards him. Ben mustered every ounce of his courage and stood his ground. What could it do? Push him over? Bite him? But when it had almost reached him, and showed no sign of stopping, his nerve broke, and he turned and ran again, nearly dashing straight into a tree trunk. He dodged off to one side, thinking that he would work his way back to the edge of the trees and so out towards the lake and the campfire. The feeble circle of light from his torch picked out wrinkled bark, leaf-strewn ground, dangling creepers, moths. Then, impossibly, the lizard's face was there, the cold reptile eyes unblinking in the halo of light, the lumbering body moving towards him.

Ben swung around and searched with his torch behind him. Yes, there were two lizards! The other one was still following, steadily, implacably. He was cut off from escape towards the campfire! He turned and moved as quickly as he could away from his pursuers, deeper into the trees. He found his voice again, and shouted out desperately as he ran, 'Help! Help!' With growing horror he realised that he must now be out of earshot of the others.

What could he do? Should he hide somewhere in the darkness with his torch extinguished? They would smell him out. Climb a tree? Normal iguanas could climb trees easily. Whatever happened, he mustn't lose his sense of direction. He must try to work his way back towards the lake. He stopped, to catch his breath and to try to form a plan of action.

Meanwhile, back at the campfire, Claire surveyed who was there. Zarina was seated a little apart with Trueno, speaking in Spanish. Uva Seca was preening his feathers beside her. The porters were washing dishes at the edge of the lake. Professor Svensson and Pierre Rabanade were deep in conversation. Anneka, Dad and Ben were nowhere to be seen. She had to speak to Ben about the brujo.

'Where's Dad and Ben?' she asked.

Professor Svensson turned to her with a kindly smile, while Pierre Rabanade poked a stick petulantly into the fire, apparently irritated by the interruption.

'Your father and the lovely Anneka are taking the first turn in the night hide by the lake,' the Professor said.

He pointed along the shore in the opposite direction to the one Claire had taken earlier.

'Your brother, I think, is perhaps with them.'

Claire thanked him and picked her way along the shoreline until she could hear voices and laughing from somewhere near the water's edge. She felt annoyed. How were they supposed to see any animals if they were making all that racket?

'Dad? Ben?' she called out.

Anneka's face poked out from a wall of rushes.

'Hey up! Here we are!'

Dad's face peered at her from over Anneka's shoulder. The moonlight glinted off his spectacles.

'Ah, there you are!' he said. 'Got Ben with you?'

'No. I thought he was with you.'

'No. Not here. Just Anneka and me. Do you want to come in?'

'What about Ben, though?' Claire said.

'He must be back at the tents,' Dad said. 'Probably asleep.'

Claire hesitated a moment. She needed to talk to Ben about Zarina and the brujo. She shuddered afresh at the memory of the winged magician, and on impulse ducked into the low doorway of the hide. She felt safer in there, snuggled up against Dad.

Claire soon fell asleep in the hide, but at some point in the night her dad was shaking her excitedly and saying, 'Ssh! Look out there, Claire, look, towards the lake!'

She looked drowsily. There, about twenty metres away in the moonlight was a creature with spotted fur about the size of a labrador dog. It was drinking with a noisy lapping of its long tongue. It had a broad whiskered muzzle and little beady eyes.

'That's it!' Anneka whispered breathlessly. 'That must be what we were eating! It's like a cross between a giant guinea-pig and a wild dog!'

Dad had his camera poked out of the hide with a long

lens. He pressed the shutter and there was a blinding flash. With a thumping of paws on the shingly beach, the creature fled.

'There's *some* evidence anyway, even if we don't manage to catch one!' Dad said. He looked at his watch.

'Nearly two o'clock. Professor Svensson will be ready to take his turn, if he hasn't decided to sleep instead. Let's head back to the tents.'

13
The Flame's Warning

Ben was in a state of terror. He had been driven deeper and deeper into the forest by an unknown number of the big lizards. They were working like a team of sheepdogs, herding him towards some destination known only to them. Every time he tried to dash off in a new direction, there would be one or more of them stalking towards him in the circle of light from his torch, their eyes fixed on his own, every crinkled fold of their reptilian faces expressing the unsaid words 'Oh no you don't!'

It was as dark as a barrel of soot. Very rarely a shaft of silver moonlight penetrated the leafy canopy and reached down to the ground, like a searching spotlight. The darkness was filled with scratchings and scutterings and whistlings and cawings and hootings. A seething darkness, as if the forest were alive with living creatures who marked his progress and scurried off to tell their fellows. And always, behind him, the steady plodding footfalls of the lizards' feet rustled in the leaves.

He went on in despair, his torch beam making a dim tunnel up ahead. Suddenly it illuminated a curtain of dangling lianas, looking as solid as a wall in front of him. He stopped, as much from exhaustion as anything else. He cast his light behind him. Lizards moved towards him in a solid line, shoulder to shoulder. There were dozens of them. He sank to his knees in helpless terror. Eaten by lizards in the Mexican jungle! What a way for a nine-year-old boy to go! He closed his eyes.

The footfalls stopped. He opened his eyes again. The lizards had come to a halt a few metres away, surrounding him on three sides. A heavy silence full of expectation fell on the forest. The whisperings and hootings were stilled. Something was going to happen. He shone his light again on the dangling lianas, the only way to go. In the glow of his torch beam, the curtain of creepers was drawn aside as if by an invisible hand. He got up off his knees and went forward. Through the gap in the lianas he could see a dim white light up ahead in the trees. An unearthly light that cast no shadows and illuminated nothing.

The darkness crowded around him. Now there was a voice. 'Come to the flame, Ben. Don't be afraid.'

Whose voice was that? It had come from inside his own head, not from outside.

'Come close to the white flame, Ben,' the voice went on. It was a deep voice, an authoritative voice. It sounded strangely familiar, although he couldn't identify it.

The voice continued. 'You understand me, Ben. I speak all languages and I take a voice from your memories to speak to you in your own tongue. Come, right up to the flame.'

It was a white, dancing flame in a small clearing. It hung in the air, fuelled by no fire, and giving out no heat. Ben stood in front of it. It flickered and gyrated hypnotically.

'This is the flame of sacred knowledge, Ben. This is the flame from which the brujos draw their powers. They are the protectors of Iguando. But they failed to stop your party from entering this sacred place. Because you are a child, you can sense the living soul of Iguando. But only dimly. Your sister even is too old. And your adult companions cannot sense it at all. All they see is new animals, things that are new to their *science*!'

There was something about the way the voice said 'science' that suggested an infinitely deep well of disapproval.

'But *you*, you apprehend that this is a living place. Iguando is the earth's greatest secret. A place where everything is a part of one living whole, everything is bound together in oneness. Today a small part of Iguando died. Yes. Today, you ate a small part of Iguando.'

Ben thought guiltily of his supper.

'And your party is bent on more destruction. You cannot tear away the limbs of Iguando without affecting the heart. That is why I have had you brought here, to tell you this: no animal must leave this place with you! You are the only member of your party with whom I can communicate. It is through you that I must work. You must persuade your group to leave Iguando, and to take nothing with you!'

Ben shook his head. 'How can I do that? No one's going to take any notice of me. They're grown-ups, zoologists...'

'You must try. For the sake of Iguando.'

'But what if they ignore me? No one's going to believe that a flame in the forest spoke to me! They'll just laugh at me!'

'You must try. For the sake of Iguando, and for the sake of all of yourselves! Go now, and do your best.'

The flame dimmed, wavered, and went out. Ben was in pitch darkness, his torch dangling in his hand making a tiny pool of light on the ground. A shiny black beetle was in the centre of the pool, looking up at him.

Beyond the curtain of lianas, only a single lizard was waiting for him. As he approached, it turned and moved off, twisting its head to look at him. As plainly as if in English it was saying, 'Follow me!' Ben trudged wearily after it as it waddled with surprising speed through the forest. His mind was too full of the flame's warning for him to have any more fear of the lizard, and he didn't trouble to worry about where it was leading him. He was sure he was being taken back to the camp, now that he had been told what he had to do.

On returning to her tent, drooping sleepily against Dad's side for support, Claire was surprised to find Ben sleeping in his clothes and boots. He seemed to be in a

73

very deep slumber, not shifting at all as she got undressed and wriggled into her sleeping bag, even though she accidentally jogged him with her elbow.

She decided that her amazing story would have to wait until the morning.

14
Rabanade Triumphant

The next morning, Ben and Claire woke late. Claire lay with her eyes still shut, listening. There was a faint *ca-ca-ca-ca-caw*! from somewhere overhead, and she thought of Anneka and her bird call imitations. Then she thought of the winged *brujo* and opened her eyes quickly, as if a huge man-bird might dive through the canvas roof at any moment and carry her away in its great beak.

But nothing of the sort occurred, and she listened again. There was no sound from any of the others outside. Then she saw a note pinned to the door flap of their tent and reached forward to get hold of it.

'*Gone looking for animals until lunch time. Stay near the camp. Trueno and the porters are here. Love, Dad.*'

Claire glanced at Ben.

'Ben! Wake up!'

'Uhh...what?'

'Wake up!'

Ben sat up, rubbing his eyes.

'What time is it?' he said.

'I don't know. We've slept in. Listen...last night... are you awake properly?'

'Oh...last night...listen...'

'No – you listen! Last night I saw something incredible.'

'So did I!'

'Ben. Shut up and listen, will you? Last night, I saw Zarina by the lake, and you know the old brujo at the village – the one you said you saw hovering?'

'Yes.'

'Well, he flew down from over the lake and talked to Zarina. Then he flew off again!'

Claire paused, to gauge Ben's amazed reaction. But he was surprisingly matter of fact about her news.

'Yes. The brujos have got something to do with protecting Iguando. I wouldn't be surprised if he wasn't warning Zarina to get us away from here.'

'What? How do you know that?'

Ben looked at Claire. Would she believe *his* story?

'Last night... I was forced into the forest...'

'Forced? Who by?'

'Giant lizards... like the one I told you about at the rocks.'

Claire nodded uncertainly. 'How did they force you?'

'They just kind of drove me along. I was frightened... and, when I was a long way into the forest... there was a white flame. And it spoke to me... it... it spoke to me in English!'

'The flame *spoke*?'

'It's hard to explain. Yes, it spoke words. It said that we were to leave Iguando and take nothing with us.'

'Take nothing?'

'No animals.'

'Ben – did you dream this? You were asleep when I came back to the tent last night.'

Ben glared at her. 'Did you dream about the brujo?'

'No!'

'Well – *believe* me then! This place isn't an ordinary place, Claire! Everything here is more alive, more intelligent...I don't know how to explain it. But we shouldn't be here.'

'Why can't your talking flame or the brujo or someone just come and tell Professor Svensson and Dad and the rest of them to go away then?'

Ben shook his head.

'Something to do with being too old, the voice said. It's because I'm a child that he...it...could speak to me.'

He looked at Claire.

'You believe me though, don't you? Now that you've seen the brujo for yourself? You'll help me, won't you?'

Claire looked at him blankly. He went on, urgently.

'Help me persuade Dad and the others to leave, and take nothing with us. You've got to help me, Claire!'

In the early afternoon, Dad and Anneka and Professor Svensson returned in triumph to the camp, bearing a box about the size of a shoe carton.

'Hello, Ben! Hello, Claire! Did you get some food?' their dad called.

'Yes thanks. Trueno did some eggs and tortillas.'

'Excellent. Come and see what we've got!'

Professor Svensson put the box down on the ground. Its lid was perforated with small holes, and from inside came a sound of scrabbling. He slid the lid open a little way, and let Ben peer inside first.

'Little gerbils!' Ben said. 'Baby ones!'

'Examine more closely their noses,' Professor Svensson suggested.

'Well, they're more pointy than gerbils,' Ben said, after looking for a moment.

'That's right! They're not gerbils at all. They're a new species of dwarf anteater! Notice the long widely-spread claws on their feet, perfect for climbing. We encountered them on the trunks of some trees in the forest, consuming ants on the surface of the bark. They have elongated tongues, in parallel with their bigger cousins.'

The Professor let Claire look, then closed up the lid again.

'I'm starving!' Anneka said. 'Let's go and see what Trueno's got for lunch, eh?'

Dad milled around with Anneka and the Professor. Ben thought he would try to get him alone to speak to him as soon as he could.

A few minutes later, as they were sitting around eating some tinned fish in a tomato sauce, Anneka, who was facing towards the forest, exclaimed, 'Good grief! Look what the cat's brought in!'

Pierre Rabanade appeared from the forest looking as if

he had been wrestling with several muddy dogs. His hair was plastered over his forehead, and there were scratches on his face and arms. But he swaggered along with his chin in the air, even though he was dragging a large sack along the ground behind him. He arrived at the logs where they were sitting and sank down on one with a sigh of exhaustion. Everyone looked expectantly at him. He had left his sack on the ground a few metres away, with a big stone holding it down at one corner. It kept bulging out in all directions, as if with a life of its own.

'Snake,' Pierre explained, pointing at the sack. 'Big snake, new to science. Rabanade Boa Constrictor.'

'Good Lord!' Professor Svensson exclaimed. '*Another* discovery, Pierre?'

'Yes. Boa constrictor family, but completely new. Bright yellow and green. Poisonous.'

'Poisonous? A boa constrictor?'

'Yes. I caught it when it had just eaten a small hog. It bit the hog in the leg. Paralysed it. Then wrapped itself around it like a normal python to squeeze it to death. Wonderful.'

Ben shuddered as he looked at Pierre Rabanade's face. He looked as if he had really enjoyed this grisly spectacle.

'How did you catch it?' he asked, not sure if he really wanted to know.

Pierre Rabanade sneered at him. 'Easy. I just waited for him to swallow the hog, so he was fat and slow. Then I grab him behind the head and get him into the sack.'

'How long is the snake, Pierre?' Anneka asked.

'Three, maybe four metres.'

'It must be very strong!'

Pierre Rabanade swelled up like a puff adder.

'Yes, very strong. But I took it by surprise, and I am very strong myself.'

'And very modest!' Claire said quietly.

'Pardon?' Pierre said. He hadn't caught the remark, but he saw that the others were smiling at it.

'And very clever, I said.' Claire smiled sweetly at him.

Pierre Rabanade nodded, lighting up a cigarette.

'Yes. It was a good capture.'

The Professor showed him the dwarf anteaters, which Pierre Rabanade looked at disdainfully before remarking that they would make a tasty snack for the Rabanade Boa Constrictor. Claire thought the Professor looked offended.

Then she caught Ben's eye. He looked very solemn, and she knew exactly what he was thinking. How on earth was he going to get these excited zoologists to leave their discoveries behind?

15
Snake Attack!

That night was a lively one by the campfire. All the adults were in high spirits over the success of the expedition. The new anteaters and the new snake were in the bag, as it were. The new frogs would be easy to collect when required. And the new giant guinea pig/dog creature was more than just a pleasant culinary memory, since they had bones, skin, and Dad's photograph of the one by the lake to prove its existence to the outside world.

Ben and Claire felt glum, listening to their excited chatter. More than once their dad turned to them and said, 'Cheer up! It might never happen!' which was particularly irritating given what they knew and he didn't. Ben felt as if he would burst like a balloon, he was so full of his secret knowledge.

They went to bed quite late. As usual, the forest seemed to wake up just as they were ready to sleep, strange cries and whoopings punctuating the night. Professor Svensson contributed to the uproar with a robust stentorian snoring.

Claire couldn't get to sleep. Ben's breathing suggested that he had managed to drop off, which made it even more frustrating. Everything was whirling around in her mind – flying magicians, giant lizards, Ben's talking flame, Zarina's secret rendezvous by the lake with the leader of the brujos, the strange new animals. She had expected Mexico to be an adventure, but this was a lot more than she had bargained for.

However, little by little, she grew drowsier and everything started to get muddled up. Rabanade's snake poked its head out of its bag and said, 'Hey up!' in Anneka's Yorkshire accent. A huge anteater swooped down from the sky on a broomstick and scattered little colourful packets of chewing gum everywhere. Uva Seca pecked them up and swallowed them, paper and all. It was all a dream, she realised. Everything that had happened was just a dream... a dream that would fade by morning... she could relax now... it would all turn out to be a dream...

She sat up with a start. She had been asleep, or very nearly asleep, but something had disturbed her. The moonlight shone on the flap at the end of the tent. A waving, weaving silhouette moved against the bright background, and a soft hissing noise seemed to be right inside her ear. A snake! A gigantic snake was inside the tent!

No horror could be more horrible than that moment! Claire's throat tightened up and she couldn't make a sound. She felt the heavy weight of the huge snake slithering across the foot of her sleeping bag, like a great rope being dragged along. Its head was poking about in the corners of the tent, then rearing up to explore the tent pole. It was only inches away from her. What would it do? Was it Rabanade's boa constrictor, escaped from its sack? Would poisonous fangs sink into her at any moment, paralysing her before she was wrapped in its coils and crushed to death?

'What's going on?'

It was Ben, who sat up suddenly in his sleeping bag, rubbing his eyes. The snake must have crawled over him and woken him up.

'Don't move!' Claire managed to croak.

Ben's eyes looked around blearily, then focused. He saw the snake. Felt it slithering across his body. Screamed his head off.

'Help! Help! Help!'

Claire saw the snake react to Ben's panic. It reared up over him, as if it might strike. Claire had no time to think. She lunged forward and caught the snake in both hands just below its head.

It transfixed her with its hideous green eyes, and hissed alarmingly, its forked tongue flickering towards her face as if it were another, smaller snake coming out of its mouth. Now she found her voice again.

'Ben! Get hold of its body! Get hold of it!'

Ben hurled himself down the tent, like a fighting caterpillar in his sleeping bag. He got hold of the snake's thrashing tail. Now what?

Just then a new shape appeared at the moonlit tent flap, and it was unzipped hurriedly.

'What's going on? Are you all right?'

It was their dad, coming to the rescue. He stuck his

head into the tent, and didn't appear to like what he saw.

'Good grief! What are you doing with that snake?'

Trust Dad to think of the snake first.

'It's not us that are doing anything with it!' Claire gasped. The snake was so strong, it was all she could do to hold it away from her. 'It came in and attacked us!'

Their dad didn't waste any more words. He climbed in and took a grip just below Claire's. Together, the three of them manoeuvred the snake out of the tent.

'It's a good job I taught you how to handle snakes at the zoo!' Dad said.

Just then, a terrible cry came out of the night.

'*Au secours! Au secours!*'

'Pierre calling for help!' Dad exclaimed. 'Now what's happening?'

The others were scrambling out of their tents. Professor Svensson wore a nightgown and tassled sleeping cap. He looked totally dumbfounded to see the Swift family grappling with a huge snake in the moonlight. Anneka was shining a torch towards Pierre's tent.

'Where is Pierre?' she said.

The Frenchman's cries were certainly not coming from his tent. In fact, they were growing fainter and fainter.

'Help!' Ben called out. The snake was curling its tail tightly around his wrists.

'Good heavens!' Anneka exclaimed, noticing the snake for the first time. She hurried across and together with Professor Svensson took over Ben's grip on it. They helped Claire and her dad to carry it over to the stacked boxes and cages. An empty sack on the ground confirmed that it was Rabanade's boa constrictor they were dealing with. Professor Svensson selected a suitable box, and they dropped the snake inside, shutting the lid quickly. It hissed angrily and thumped about inside.

By the time the snake had been put away, Pierre Rabanade's cries had faded away completely. Ben had been listening carefully though, and was certain of one thing. It was something that he would only be able to tell Claire. The cries had definitely been coming from the sky!

16
A Risky Disclosure

No one slept very much for the remainder of that night, and it was a tired dishevelled group that gathered around the campfire in the morning to drink Trueno's sugary tea, and eat tortillas with refried beans.

Claire kept glancing at Zarina as they ate. She hadn't scrambled out of her tent last night when the others did. She had somehow appeared on the scene from nowhere, when the snake was being put in the box. Now she was silent and preoccupied, and twice Claire thought she saw her looking quickly upwards, as if checking something. Uva Seca perched on the log beside her, pecking at a plate of titbits with a doleful air.

Various theories were put forward as to what had happened to Pierre Rabanade. The suggestion that he had wandered into the forest in the night and met with some misadventure was considered probable until Anneka pointed out that his boots were sitting under the door flap of his tent.

'He wouldn't have gone wandering off without his boots, would he?' she said.

Professor Svensson seemed paralysed by the mystery. He shook his head and looked around vaguely with unfocused eyes and tugged at his beard and muttered things like, 'This is really most disconcerting!'

Zarina wasn't saying anything at all, except in a low voice to Uva Seca, and after a shared glance with Anneka, Dad took it upon himself to assume the mantle of leadership.

'We need to organise a search, boots or no boots. Three parties: Zarina – could you go with Trueno and Juan and José northwards along the shore of the lake? Professor Svensson and Anneka – would you go south along the lake? The children and myself will go into the forest to the east. To the west is the lake, and if he's in there, there's nothing to be done about it. I suggest we limit our search to one mile approximately from the camp, and then come back.'

Claire looked at Dad with a little surprise. She hadn't been aware of this masterful, leadership quality in him. His spectacles glinted with cool-headed determination, and the bristles of his beard stood to attention like a hedgehog's prickles, ready to repel any attack.

The search parties set off. Dad got Ben and Claire to form a line with him, keeping about twenty metres apart. Then they headed into the trees, occasionally shouting out, 'Pierre!'

The children couldn't really shout with any conviction. They were sure they knew what had really happened to Rabanade, but it seemed impossible to broach the subject with Dad. Ben turned over and over in his mind what he might say, but he could imagine only too clearly the blank stare of incredulity this hard-headed search-party organiser would give him if he suggested that the object of their hunt had been carried off by flying wizards.

About a mile away from the camp they came to the open hillside with the big rocks at the top where they had made a hide.

'We'll go as far as the top of this,' Dad said. 'Then we'd better go back.'

From the top of the hill, they scanned the landscape. Claire was struck by the clarity of the air today. The mountains which surrounded Iguando seemed to have marched closer. They loomed over the rolling forest like jagged jaws about to close. Huge clouds were massed over the serrated peaks, and she thought she could just hear a distant rumble of thunder from far beyond the horizon. A shiver ran down her spine.

Back at the camp, neither of the other search parties had returned. Dad yawned and rubbed his eyes.

'I'm going to have a little siesta in my tent. I need it after last night. What about you two?'

Ben and Claire shook their heads. They were too worried to sleep.

'All right. Don't go away from the camp site though. We've got to be careful now.'

Dad crawled into his tent, and Ben and Claire sat on some rocks by the lake's edge. A wind had sprung up, and the water was ruffled into white spikes of foam.

'I wonder if the brujos dropped Pierre Rabanade in the middle of the lake,' Claire said.

Ben shrugged. He felt worn out by the tension between needing to tell Dad what he knew, and the fear that he would just be laughed at and ignored. They sat on in silence for a while.

'What about Zarina?' Claire said after a few minutes.

'What about her?'

'I bet we could get her to persuade them to leave! Especially when they don't find any sign of Pierre Rabanade today.'

'Why should we trust her though?' Ben objected. 'If she finds out what we know, she might just have us flown off into the night as well!'

'But she was arguing with the leader of the brujos. I bet she's not all bad. I think she'd help us get away.'

'I don't know. I'm frightened of her.'

'So am I. But if we don't talk to her, who knows what's going to happen?'

Ben looked at the ominous dark clouds over the distant mountains.

'This place is starting to give me the creeps! I just want to go,' he said.

Just then he caught a glimpse of movement along the edge of the lake to the north. It was Zarina and Trueno and the two porters returning to camp. He pointed them out to Claire.

'Well, they won't have bothered searching,' she said. 'I expect they've spent the morning somewhere just out of sight of the camp.'

The four figures slowly grew nearer. When they

reached the campfire, Trueno and the porters stopped, and they could faintly hear Trueno's voice, presumably giving orders to do with water, or firewood, or something.

Zarina carried on towards her own tent, where Uva Seca was perching asleep on the ridge pole. She didn't appear to have noticed the children. But Ben waved an arm in the air and called out.

'Zarina!'

Claire grabbed his arm to pull it down.

'No! We need to talk this through first!' she hissed.

But it was too late. Zarina was walking towards them, her long black skirt and loose jet hair billowing in the wind. She looked like a sleek raven, about to take flight.

'Hello, you two!' she said. 'Did you find anything?'

Claire glanced at Ben. He looked petrified. Swallowing a lump in her throat, she spoke as boldly as she could.

'No. But then we wouldn't find anything *on the ground*, would we?'

Zarina looked at her sharply. 'What do you mean?'

Ben spoke up. He could see Claire's lip trembling.

'She means we know what happened to Pierre! He was carried away by the brujos!'

Zarina stared at them, one at a time, as if assessing how best to exterminate them. Her loose fitting clothes flapped like wings about her body. Claire felt her nerve about to crack. In a moment she would scream and run away...

90

17
Revelations

However, after her long stare, Zarina glanced around and spoke in a low voice, as if there might be an invisible listener lurking somewhere.

'I should not have expected you to be blind to the magic of this place. Adults go around with their eye closed by half, but you do not.'

'So we're right then, aren't we?' Ben said. 'Pierre was taken by the brujos?'

'Yes.'

'But why?'

Zarina looked up at the sky, where big clouds were crowding the sun, big grey pillows of moisture, edged with light.

'Please tell us. We want to understand what's going on.'

Zarina looked at them again, as if unable to make up her mind. Then she nodded.

'Very well. I will try to explain what is our situation. It was starting for me when the Mexican government has agreed to the zoological expedition in this area. They make me a job as liaison officer for the expedition. This job was to have organise everything in this place for them. But as well as to satisfy the government, also I had to satisfy the leaders of the brujos in our community.'

Zarina looked at them again. Claire thought she was wondering how much to tell them. After a moment, she went on.

'You have to understand that there are sacred animals in this country, and the most sacred of all of them all, they are here, in Iguando. The brujos, they say to me that I have to keep the expedition away from this place – at every cost.

'When the party is first arriving in Tepestloatan, I showed maps to Professor Svensson. I showed him good places to come, in the south. Far away from here. But he has to insist to come to the hills, to the west and north of Tepestloatan. The best I can do was to guide him to the camp on the old logging road, which was still well away from Iguando. Also, as you are now knowing, it is not easy to find the way to Iguando from that place.

'But I didn't know about Pierre Rabanade. Later I find out that he has been here before, in this part of Mexico. Perhaps he hears legends of a secret place, where the animals are like no others. While I am away to Mexico City collecting you from the airport, he is paying one of the porters to show him the way here.'

'The money!' Claire exclaimed. 'I saw you making Juan and José eat bank notes the first night we were here!'

Zarina smiled wryly. 'You have good eyes in the darkness, Claire Swift!'

Claire looked away across the water, embarrassed.

'Anyway, yes. It is true. I make them eat the money they had earned by this treachery. But that was the smallest punishment I could make them. Amargor, the leader of the brujos, he was in a very big anger with me, as well as the porters. You have to understand that although I too am a bruja, we are not all the same in our beliefs. I am belonging to the Brujeria Benigna. We worship the same sacred animals as the Brujeria Amarga, but with one difference, very important. We believe that the human life is as sacred as that of our gods. But the Brujeria Amarga, they place the human life – how would you say? – lower in the scales. To protect the secret of Iguando, they would kill. Juan and José were lucky to live.'

'We saw you arguing with the brujo at Tepestloatan, after the dance,' Ben said. 'Was that Amargor?'

'Yes,' Zarina nodded. 'That was him.'

'And beside the lake two nights ago – was that him again?' Claire asked.

Zarina flashed a look of surprise at her.

'Again you see sharp in the night!' she said. 'Yes, he has come to speak to me then. He warned me that the patience of the spirit animals, it was almost all gone away. A storm was coming that would destroy you all unless I can get you to go from Iguando.'

'Why did they take Pierre?' Claire asked.

Zarina shook her head. 'That I don't know. Perhaps as a final warning. I was also surprised as you.'

'And the snake in our tent?' Ben said. 'Was that meant to kill us?'

Zarina looked at him steadily. 'Possibly, yes. I think Amargor, he is getting desperate now.'

'So, we should get out of here as soon as we can!'
Claire said.

'Yes,' Zarina agreed. 'It's what I have to make to
happen now, before it's too late. I have to get these
zoologists to come away. But they are all scientists. How
could they be paying any attention to tales of magic?'

'Can you fly?' Ben said suddenly.

A smile crossed Zarina's face as quickly as a wind-
driven cloud. 'To convince them of magic and persuade
them to leave? No. It is not so easy to do. There are
rituals to act out, a special potion to be brewed with rare
plants taken from different parts of the forest. I can't just
fly up into the air – how do you say it in English? – at
the drop of the hat!'

'But Amargor – he can fly when he wants?'

'Amargor, he is the most powerful brujo of our
people. He has powers which are a lot more than mine.
And he is angry now. Also he is very afraid.'

'*Amargor* is afraid?'

'Yes. He is afraid of the god of Iguando.'

18
A Disagreement

In the middle of the afternoon the third search party – Professor Svensson and Anneka – could be seen approaching the camp along the edge of the lake from the south. Something seemed to be moving along a hundred metres or so behind them. A small lump, close to the ground. An animal of some sort perhaps, it was hard to be sure.

When they drew near, Anneka's face was flushed with excitement. She pointed backwards.

'A lizard! It's followed us all day! Like an iguana, but bigger. It must be like the one you saw, is it, Ben?'

Ben nodded. The lizard was rather smaller and lighter looking than the ones he had encountered, but appeared to be of the same type. Perhaps it was a young one.

'Most strange,' Professor Svensson confirmed, mopping his brow. 'I have never come across a reptile of such a persistent disposition. It is undoubtedly a new species. We must endeavour to capture it.'

Zarina stood up suddenly. 'No! We have done enough! The lizard especially is sacred to this place. This one is sent to watch us.'

Professor Svensson, Anneka and Mike Swift goggled at Zarina, lower jaws dangling as if someone had just cut the strings. If she had announced that pigs could fly to the moon, they could not have looked more incredulous.

'Sent to watch us?' Professor Svensson spluttered. 'Sent? A lizard? Who would *send* a lizard anywhere, and how would the lizard *know* it was sent?'

Zarina's mouth was a hard line, her lips blood red. She shook her head. Claire thought she had said more than she had meant to, and wished it unsaid.

'I mean that we should respect the beliefs of my people. The lizards of this place, they are not ordinary animals.'

'No. Most definitely not,' Professor Svensson agreed. 'That is why they are important to science. We must have one to take back. Or more, if possible, so that they can be bred in captivity.'

They all looked over to where the lizard had stopped, about fifty metres away. It was looking at them. Zarina seemed about to say more, but obviously decided against it. The Professor stroked his beard a few times, as if stoking a fire, and addressed them.

'Well, the question of the lizard we can return to. It looks as if it is not going away. First, to our other problem. Now, thank you, everyone, for your efforts today to detect our esteemed colleague Pierre Rabanade. I presume that you, like us, have drawn the blanket?'

'Drawn a blank, Professor,' Dad said, nodding.

'Thank you. Then his subtraction from our presence remains a mystery.' He paused a moment and looked glum, as if holding a private brief memorial service. Then his face brightened.

96

'On the positive side, we have made a good commencement to our collection, which now comprises the dwarf anteaters; the bones and fur of our lamented supper of two nights ago; and, of course, the Rabanade Boa Constrictor – a fitting memorial to our French friend should he, tragically, fail to turn up again. I will also this afternoon collect specimens of the new species of frog from the lake's margins' – Here he looked up briefly over the top of his glasses – 'the *Svensson* frog.'

This summary of the state of affairs seemed to satisfy the Professor, for he smiled pleasantly. The loss of a French zoologist was clearly more than compensated for by the gain of so many specimens new to science.

'But Professor,' Dad said, stroking his own beard for inspiration, 'surely we should report the loss of Pierre Rabanade to the authorities as soon as possible?'

The Professor looked uncertain. Zarina chipped in.

'That is right. It is, in fact, required by Mexican law. We must leave tomorrow, and report how he is vanished at Tepestloatan.'

Ben and Claire looked at Zarina, then back to the Professor. The bit about Mexican law sounded like an invention of her own, but it might work. They knew she was as desperate as they were to get everyone out of Iguando.

'Well...' The Professor was shaking his head uncertainly. He had the expression of a boy with his hand halfway down a deep bag of sweets who has been told to stop eating or it will spoil his supper.

'I agree,' their dad chimed in. 'It doesn't seem right just to carry on when Pierre's vanished into thin air. Who knows what dangers there might be here? I think we should go back tomorrow.' He turned to Anneka. 'What do you think, Anneka?'

Anneka nodded. 'Aye – it's the right thing to do. Perhaps the Mexican police could come in here with a proper search party.'

Claire glanced towards Zarina. She didn't think the brujos would like that idea. But Zarina was nodding, to encourage Anneka's support for the proposal to leave.

Professor Svensson scanned the faces of Zarina, Anneka and Dad for a moment. Then he shook his head sadly. 'Well, I have no choice since you are all in accordance. We will embark tomorrow morning for our original base camp, and then regress to Tepestloatan immediately in our vehicles.'

'The animals should be released before we go,' Zarina said, confronting the Professor with a steely, Gorgon-like stare. But he did not turn to stone. Instead he went red in the face, and scowled.

'I think, Zarina, that I shall be the judge of all matters pertaining to the animals. That is my part in the expedition I think? There is no question of leaving them here!' He glanced towards Dad and Anneka, who nodded their agreement on this point. 'And what is more' – He gestured towards the lizard, which still stood about fifty metres away – 'I am going to add to our collection right now. Trueno! José! Juan!'

The cook and the porters came over at his call from where they were preparing supper. Dad and Anneka stood up to help as well. Striding to the supply tent, the Professor beckoned them to follow, and delved inside for lengths of rope, which he distributed to them. All his customary dithering had vanished, and he was transformed into a man of action.

The Professor had not earned his reputation as a zoologist for nothing. With impressive cunning and expertise, he directed his assistants to approach the lizard from all directions, while he himself got close enough to cast a big net over it. Within minutes they had the creature off its feet, in spite of its strength. They carried it in the net between them to the biggest of the collapsible cages, and thrust it in.

Zarina made no attempt to interfere, and indeed turned half away, looking up into the sky over the lake. But Uva Seca, who stood beside her, shook his head.

'Bad!' the parrot squawked. 'Very very bad!'

There was a bustle of activity in the camp for the next few hours. As far as possible, everything was to be packed and made ready for the morning's journey before darkness fell. Professor Svensson went off along the lake's edge and collected some frogs, as he had promised. As night approached, the sky filled with great clouds, piled up to an enormous height like leaning towers, all ready to tumble down on top of them. Black vultures wheeled about in the lowering space beneath the clouds. Occasionally there was a deep boom of thunder in the distant mountains, as if a giant was beating on a vast kettledrum. The wind, which had been hot earlier, quickly turned cold, and soon after supper big drops of rain began to fall like wet coins, making the bonfire fizzle and smoulder, and driving them all to the shelter of their tents.

19
Another Disappearance

'I'll be glad when morning comes!' Claire said to Ben as they lay wide awake. She had to speak quite loudly, even though they were right next to each other. The rain was beating on the canvas roof of their tent, and thunder was rumbling threateningly in the distance.

'What's the time now?' Ben said.

Claire consulted her watch. 'Half past twelve!'

'You know what I've decided we've got to do, Claire?'

'What?'

'We've got to try to release the animals in the night, while everyone's asleep.'

Claire considered this.

'Haven't you noticed how they're kept?'

'What do you mean?'

'Professor Svensson has everything locked up. Even the frogs and the little anteaters are inside padlocked boxes. I saw him putting them in his tent. And he's got the big boxes – with the snake and the lizard – chained together. He's not taking any chances, after Pierre Rabanade disappearing and Zarina saying we should let them go.'

'We could get his keys,' Ben said.

'Get real! How? We don't know where he keeps them. Probably inside his sleeping bag!'

'Well...' Ben started to scramble into his jeans. '...I don't care how difficult it is, I've got to try. The flame said I had to do my best. Are you going to help or not?'

'All right, I'll help you!' Claire said, attempting not to sound as hopeless as she felt.

They got their clothes on and slipped into their boots. Outside the tent, their feet made loud sucking noises in the muddy ground, but fortunately there was a lot of covering sound from the rain and thunder.

When they got to Professor Svensson's tent, they peeped cautiously through the mosquito netting. It was too dark to see anything.

'I'll have to shine my torch in,' Ben said. 'If it wakes him up, it's too bad. We can't look for his keys in the dark, with him lying there.'

But Ben's torch revealed a surprise. The Professor's sleeping bag was empty, like a sloughed-off snake skin. Where was he?

'Oh no!' Ben breathed. 'Don't say the brujos have got him!'

'He may have just popped out for a pee!' Claire suggested. 'We'd better search while we can!'

They unzipped the flap and crawled in. The tent was even untidier than their own, with clumps of sweaty old clothes lying about everywhere like fungus.

'Yuk!' Claire said fastidiously. 'We might catch some disease in here!'

'Never mind that. Here are the boxes with the frogs and the dwarf anteaters at the back. Look for the keys.'

102

'He's probably got them with him.'

'Never mind, just look, will you!'

They rooted about frantically. Reluctantly Claire poked a hand down into the greasy interior of the empty sleeping bag. There was a little chink of metal, and her fingers closed around a cold bunch of keys.

'Yes! I was right! That's where I would have kept them – but only as long as I was in the sleeping bag too.'

Claire withdrew her hand from the bag and dangled the keys triumphantly in front of Ben.

At that very moment there was a sudden loud squelch from outside the tent door, and a powerful beam of light dazzled them. Ben half expected to hear 'Police! Lay down your weapons and put your hands in the air!'

But instead there was the unique and unmistakable sound of a Swedish Professor of Zoology expressing a mixture of surprise, anger and triumph.

'A-haaargh! I thought there would be an attempt to abduct my precious specimens under nocturnal cover! Yes! I thought so! But you? No, I did not think to find those so young involved in this dreadful crime!'

This was quite a long speech in the circumstances, and neither Ben nor Claire had much to say in reply.

'It is Zarina that has put this up you, no? It is her doing, all this, yes?'

'No...' Ben began. Just then there was another squelch from behind the Professor, and Dad's voice made itself heard.

'What's going on, Professor?'

'My dear friend. I have to impart to you, more in sadness than in anger, that your offspring are in my tent!'

'In your tent? Ben! Claire! Are you in there?'

'Yes,' Claire said in a small voice.

'Well come out right now! What's going on?'

The children crawled out into the rain. Professor Svensson answered on their behalf.

'I knew I had to be on my guard tonight! I was out to check on the larger specimens, which I was doing every half hour, and when I returned, I found that an attempt was being made to subtract our precious frogs and anteaters!'

'Surely not!' Dad exclaimed. 'Claire, Ben . . . you must have had some other reason for being in the Professor's tent?'

Ben looked at Claire.

'Go on, Ben!' she encouraged him. 'Ben has something to tell you, Dad.'

'Come into my tent then. There's no point in us all getting any more soaked than we are already out here! Professor, do you want to hear this?'

But Professor Svensson barged grumpily into his tent, like an old badger. He spoke over his shoulder.

'No. I am not going to leave my specimens at the mercy of another marauder. I am staying in here. This is all dirty work by that woman Zarina!'

The Swift family retired to Dad's tent.

'Now then?' Dad said sternly.

Ben took a deep breath and told his father about the

lizards, his journey through the forest at night, the white dancing flame and its warning.

Then Claire told him about what Zarina had said, and about Amargor the brujo, and how Pierre Rabanade had been carried away into the sky.

Their dad, who had at first asked questions, fell increasingly silent, fiddling uneasily with the zip of his sleeping bag.

'So you see,' Ben said as soon as Claire had finished, 'we mustn't take anything away with us from Iguando! It would be dangerous and it would just be...wrong! This place has to remain secret, or people will come here and destroy it all!'

Dad still didn't say anything. Claire took his hand in hers.

'Dad! I know you must be thinking we've gone mad, or we're having crazy dreams or something. But please try to believe us! It's so important!'

'I can't,' their dad said at last, avoiding their eyes. 'None of this makes any sense at all. I know Iguando is different. Of course I can feel that too. And the amazing wildlife here proves that it's different. But we can't just forget that we ever discovered this place! We can't release our animals and go home and pretend that we never came here! Whatever dreams you've been having – and I'm sorry to say that I can only call them dreams – it would be against all the principles of science just to turn away from this extraordinary place and pretend to the world that we never found it!'

A big tear rolled down Ben's cheek. He couldn't help it. His dad looked guilty and pulled him towards him to give him a hug.

'Ben! Ben! I'm sorry.'

'Dad!' Claire said. 'What if Zarina backed up our story? Would you believe us then?'

'Zarina?'

'Yes. She knows this is all true. Come on – let's go to her tent, and she'll tell you!'

'I really don't think ...'

'Come on!'

Shaking his head, Dad followed them to Zarina's tent.

'Zarina!' Claire called softly, before bending to look in through the mosquito netting. Then she gasped in dismay.

'What is it?' Ben said, leaning past her to look in.

The tent was completely empty.

Zarina and Uva Seca had gone!

20
On the Run!

The rest of the night was terrible. The rain fell on Claire and Ben's tent as if hundreds of tiny claws were trying to stab their way through the roof. The thunder stalked nearer and nearer, and louder and louder, changing from a rolling drum-like sound to a fierce, brittle, cracking noise right overhead, as if monsters were smashing up huge wooden boxes and hurling them to the ground. Lightning periodically lit up the landscape outside, so that it appeared like a vivid picture through the canvas wall of the tent, a silvery wild scene of raging water and swaying trees. Ben turned restlessly from side to side, while in his mind he turned over the significance of Zarina abandoning them. Eventually he fell into an uneasy sleep. Meanwhile, Claire had nightmares of beating wings and cries for help.

When a murky grey dawn light began to seep into their tent they woke up more tired than when they had gone to bed. However, the nightmares of their sleep were nothing compared with what awaited them outside.

Ben was the first to poke his head out of the door of their tent. He gasped in dismay.

'What is it?' Claire said.

'The camp – everything's gone!'

107

'What!'

'The other tents, the animals, everyone! They've all gone!'

Claire pushed past him and looked for herself.

'Oh...'

She looked at the empty space to their left where Dad's tent had been.

'Dad! Oh, Ben – what's happened to Dad!'

They looked at each other for a moment, eyes filling with tears, then clutched each other tightly and sobbed.

'The brujos...the brujos must have come in the night,' Claire gasped out after a few minutes.

After the first wave of anguish had swept over them, they dabbed their faces dry and sat for a while in stunned silence. Ben spoke first.

'What are we going to do?'

Claire stared blankly in front of her.

'I don't know. I can't think. Wait here until the brujos come back for us?'

'But why did they leave us? Why did they take everyone else – and all the equipment – and leave us?'

'I don't know. So we could suffer?'

'There must be a reason. Maybe Zarina...'

'Zarina is one of them. She'd already gone off last night. She's no better than the rest of them.'

'But Zarina knew we were trying to help. The flame said to me that I should do my best. We did do our best – didn't we? We tried to release the animals.'

Claire nodded. 'It didn't help though, did it?'

'But perhaps if we'd succeeded, they might not have taken everyone away. Maybe they're giving us a last chance. Maybe there's something we can do, to save everyone?'

'Or maybe we can only save ourselves now,' Claire said mournfully. 'Oh, poor Dad!'

'Well, we've got to do something, haven't we?' Ben said, fighting down the impulse to cry again. 'We've got to look for them, or something.'

'But where should we look? We'd just get lost in the jungle. Then we'd end up starving to death.'

They stared into space for a little while longer. The situation seemed so hopeless, they felt numbed. Claire even thought about getting back into her sleeping bag and trying to go to sleep. Perhaps she would wake up to find this had all been a nightmare.

Ben spoke up at last.

'I think we should set off back the way we came into Iguando – towards the first camp. If we could get back to there, then we could follow the road back to Zarina's village. That's where the brujos come from. That's the only place where we might get help. They might even have taken Dad and everyone back there.'

Claire thought about it. It was better than no plan at all.

'Okay. I can sort of remember the direction we came from, when we came down from the ridge through that horrible bat cave.'

'Should we carry our tent?'

109

'No point. If we can get back to the first camp by nightfall, there's a tent there, remember?'

'There *was* a tent there. The brujos might have taken that too.'

'Well, let's leave it anyway. It'll only slow us down.'

They got their cagoules on and packed up their rucksacks. Ben found a packet of biscuits unexpectedly, so they at least had something for breakfast.

'Mum must have put these in for the journey,' Ben said through a mouthful of crumbs.

'I wonder what she'd have thought if she could have known what state we'd be in when we were eating them!'

'She'd have kept us at home. I wish we were at home!'

'But not without Dad?'

'No, not without Dad.'

The rain had eased off now, and steamy moisture rose from the soaking forest trees, and lay in a thin mist over the surface of the lake. The two of them set off along the shore, heading south. Beyond the forest, in the distance, lay the ridge of hills from which they had descended into Iguando. At the end of the lake, Ben turned back to look one last time at the empty scene, hoping, in spite of everything, to see Dad and Anneka and Professor Svensson emerge miraculously from the trees and wave a greeting to them. But the shore remained stubbornly deserted, and instead Ben's eyes were drawn upwards to the sky, where huge dark clouds were gathering afresh over the jagged mountains to the north. Lightning stabbed downwards as he watched, lighting up one of the rocky peaks in blue fire, and a few seconds later a roll of thunder, the first since dawn, reached their ears.

'Oh no! Not more rain storms,' Claire groaned. 'Aren't we wet enough already?'

They trudged onwards into the forest beyond the lake, and the ground soon began to rise gradually. There was no clear path to follow, but the vegetation was sparse beneath the forest canopy, and Claire checked her compass from time to time to ensure they kept heading south. Behind them they could hear the storm getting closer, and it grew so dark that it seemed as if night was going to fall again.

It was then that the drumming began.

At first it was mixed in with the low rumbling of distant thunder. But gradually Ben became aware that there was a rhythm in the deep sound. Boom, boom, boom, boom! A pause. Then again: boom, boom, boom, boom! It seemed to be coming from behind them. He looked at Claire.

'Do you hear that?' he said.

Claire's face was white. 'Yes. What to you think it is?'

'I don't know what. But it might be something following us!'

'Let's go faster anyway!'

They scrambled onwards in the growing gloom.

Then the eyes began.

It was Claire who saw them first. Little glinting specks in the gloom, little flickering pairs of lights that vanished as soon as she tried to focus on them. There! Off to the side! No...they were gone.

'Claire...'

'Yes?'

'Do you keep seeing eyes?'

'Yes. We're being watched, aren't we?'

'Yes. I don't like this.'

'Me neither.'

They broke into a trot. Perhaps up ahead, where the trees were thinner, they would be able to see more clearly. There, they would be able to defend themselves better from any attack...

Then the pattering began.

It was a soft patter-pat-pat on the leaves of the forest floor. Claire would have thought it was raindrops, but no rain was falling. Like the drumming, which was growing gradually louder, it seemed to be coming from behind them. Ben cast a look over his shoulder.

'There's something behind us, Claire. Can you see anything?'

'No – it's so gloomy. But I can hear something. Is it footsteps?'

'Must be a lot of them. Sounds like hundreds of footsteps on the leaves.'

'Let's run!'

21
Gliding Like Vultures

Ben and Claire ran at full tilt through the trees. They broke out of the forest onto a rock-strewn slope. It rose in front of them to the high ridge that marked the southern edge of Iguando. Looking back into the trees, Claire could still see winking little eyes, and hear the pattering rush of pursuing feet. The boom, boom, boom, boom! of the drums rumbled out of the sky and the earth, surrounding them with its insistent rhythm. They paused, gasping for breath, and suddenly a winged shape flashed past their eyes and landed on a great cracked boulder nearby.

'Ben! Claire!' came a gruff croaking cry, and with a flap of his green wings Uva Seca lifted up again into the sky, and flew off towards the ridge.

'Uva Seca!' Ben exclaimed. 'Do you think Zarina sent him to find us?'

'I hope so!' Claire replied.

In spite of everything, the appearance of the parrot had lifted their spirits. Perhaps they were not entirely alone in their peril? Perhaps they had not been entirely abandoned?

They scrambled upwards in the direction that Uva Seca had taken and soon came to the banks of a fast-flowing river. Its noisy tumbling water drowned out the sound of pattering feet in the forest, but the deep booming sound still vibrated in the air.

'There he goes!' Ben cried, pointing at a flash of green and red far upstream. 'He wants us to follow him up this river.'

'What if he's leading us into a trap?' Claire said.

'I don't care, as long as Dad's there. Uva Seca must know where everyone is.'

They followed the bird as the river became narrower and steeper. After a while they found themselves in a canyon, with steep rocky cliffs looming over them on both sides. The canyon narrowed and narrowed until finally they were confronted by a dark gash sliced into a towering rock face ahead of them as if by a giant's blow with an enormous axe.

The cleft was filled with the sound of cascading water, and in the gloom Ben could just make out the silvery flash of a huge waterfall. Uva Seca flew up and over the top of the rock face, and out of sight. At the same time, rain began to fall, heavily, from the leaden black sky.

'That's great!' Claire said, pulling on the hood of her cagoule. 'He's led us into a dead end. Now what?'

'Well, there's no point in going back now. Perhaps there's a way through. Like the bat cave – a way up through the rock.'

They edged forward to investigate the dark chasm ahead. There was something strange in there, silhouetted against the silvery flash of the waterfall. A line of thick dripping rope, strung across the gorge, with something suspended from it. Boxes? Or cages...

Claire suddenly grabbed Ben's arm painfully.

'Ow! What...'

'Ben – look in those cages! Look! It's Professor Svensson!'

'And Anneka! The porters...'

'And Dad! Look! In the end one!'

Swinging in the suspended wooden cages high above the raging river were the members of the expedition. They were all slumped, silent, as if dead, in their cramped prisons.

'And look – at the other end!' Ben pointed. In the last cage there was a lanky soaking figure with its long limbs curled around its body like a serpent.

'Pierre Rabanade!' Claire exclaimed. 'So this is where they brought him!'

'Why have they done this? Why have they hung them up there from that rope?' Ben said, outraged.

Just then a deafening boom of thunder rolled out from the black sky overhead, and the children lifted their heads. Then, instinctively, Ben reached out and clutched the sleeve of Claire's cagoule in a fierce grip.

Out of the pelting rain and storm-tossed sky came winged shapes, gliding like vultures. There were dozens of them, and their wings were made of woven cloth and their painted faces were human.

'The brujos!' he gasped.

The brujos were uttering terrifying shrill bird-like calls as they floated closer and closer to the earth. Ben turned to Claire.

'What do you think? Run?'

Claire pointed a trembling finger down the valley. A great crowd of dark shapes lurked there, half obscured by the rocks and the pelting rain. Whether they were human or animal or supernatural it was impossible to say. But one thing was certain. They were there to cut off all escape in that direction.

By now the brujos were coming down to earth all around them.

Then Zarina walked out of the shadow of the rocky defile in front of them and stood with head bowed and arms crossed over her chest in a curious ritualistic pose. Uva Seca hopped out of the shadows behind her and peered around the edge of her skirts.

'Zarina must have been waiting here for us!' Claire said to Ben.

Although her head was lowered, Zarina's eyes shone like dark jewels under her fringe of hair, and watched unblinking as Amargor, the Chief of the brujos landed in front of her and struck the ground fiercely three times with a gnarled staff.

'*Axuatolotl iguando ixesis fragil abarda!*' he screamed, gesturing at the caged prisoners. He shook the rain from his cloak like a bird drying its feathers.

Zarina replied in the same high-pitched tongue. It was like hearing two herring gulls fighting over a fish.

The other brujos had all landed now, and stood in a large semi-circle around Ben and Claire. Their faces were inscrutable behind thick layers of green and white daub. Only their eyes and teeth identified them as human beings. There was something bird-like about them even on the ground. They stood with slightly arched legs, as if ready to take flight again at a moment's notice. Many of them grasped thin twisted staffs of wood with carved heads. Their fingernails were long and green, like talons. Their attention was fixed on Zarina and Amargor.

Thunder and lightning was right overhead now, the rain coming down with a force that made Claire feel the sky was trying to pound her down into the earth.

'What do you think they're saying?' she shouted to Ben over the drumming rainfall.

'I don't know,' he replied. He didn't like the way Amargor kept pointing at the cages, stabbing viciously in their direction with his gnarled stick.

The debate between Zarina and the high priest of the brujos had ascended to a pitch of frenzy. Two squawking pterodactyls could not have made more noise. Suddenly Amargor struck his staff into the ground one more time, and a great boom of thunder crashed overhead as he did so. A bolt of lightning struck a solitary tree about a hundred metres away, and it flamed like a torch. A great jolt of electricity sizzled along the ground and made Claire's legs tingle. She staggered and clutched Ben, whose hair was standing up like a brush under his hood.

Zarina once again adopted the ritualistic position, arms crossed over her chest. The circle of the brujos grew tighter. Amargor made a gesture to Zarina, and she spoke loudly to the assembled brujos in the strange Ixuatal tongue. Then she came forward and spoke to the children more quietly.

'No animals can be taken away from Iguando. It is the law of this land, sacred and not possible for changing. Your party has tried to break this solemn law. These are my people, the brujos of Tepestloatan, the protectors of Iguando. I am all failed in my task of keeping you to not discover the secrets of this place. Now the god of Iguando must be asked what is our fate.'

22
A Flame out of Water

'Our fate?' Claire said. She felt a sudden breathlessness. Ben had gone as pale as a ghost.

'Yes. Whether or not you – and I – must die for our crime! Come with me now.'

Zarina held out her hands. The children stepped forward and took them. They were icy cold.

She led them up the canyon towards the waterfall. They passed beneath the line of dangling cages. Looking up quickly, Ben could see that the occupants were completely motionless.

'Are they still alive?' he managed to croak out to Zarina. She nodded. 'For now. They are in a sleep with drugs. They know nothing of all of this. If they must be to die, they will feel no pain.'

Claire glanced back as they moved into the dark chasm. Shapes were detaching themselves from the tumbled rocks, moving forward into the open behind them. She thought she saw lizards.

The noise of the waterfall hurt your ears. It bounced off the hard cliff walls in a kind of never-ending applause of stony hands. The spray filled the air, combining with the still falling rain to make the place like one vast shower cubicle. Claire felt that she was turning to water, that she was dissolving completely in this element that engulfed them.

They came to a halt on a rocky ledge some fifty metres from the great curtain of falling water. Zarina detached her hands from theirs, and faced the waterfall. She half turned to Amargor, who, followed by the rest of the brujos, had come up the canyon behind them. Now Amargor came forward to stand next to Zarina. Striking his staff three times on the rock, he cried out with a supernaturally powerful voice, at a volume beyond the capability of human lungs.

'Iguando! Iguando! Iguando!'

There was a pause. Zarina told the children to get down on their knees, facing the waterfall. The uneven surface of the rock was painful to kneel on. Then Zarina and the brujos themselves, including Amargor, knelt also. For a few moments, nothing happened. The rain pounded down. The silvery cascade of the waterfall thundered into its pool in front of them. Ben shifted his weight uncomfortably from knee to knee.

Then a deep, deep sound came from somewhere. Deeper than thunder, deeper than an avalanche, the deepest sound there could ever be. A sound that was felt rather than heard. A sound that filled the hollows of your bones with vibrations, that rumbled in your brain and made your heart and lungs and liver jiggle about inside your body.

Then a change came to the waterfall. Behind the plunging liquid curtain, a sort of glow appeared – a pale

120

white effulgence. Between the light and the water, an unimaginably vast shape was moving. A dark shadow a hundred metres tall was cast on the silver surface. It was not a human shape, nor was it a lizard shape. But it was partly both.

Ben gasped aloud. Claire shuffled against him instinctively. All they could do was die with those they loved. An image of his mum flitted like a butterfly in and out of Ben's mind, before his attention was seized again with the awesome horror of what was unfolding in front of him.

The shape had stopped behind the curtain of water. It was a vague silhouette only. But now a huge arm reached forwards, and a single claw penetrated the waterfall and pointed, glistening, at Zarina.

Zarina scrambled to her feet and approached the edge of the pool at the foot of the waterfall. Claire couldn't imagine doing that. Walking deliberately towards such a thing.

Again the deep rumbling sound came. It might have been that there were words in the sound, but not words that you could distinguish. The syllables formed inside your head, not in the air outside.

The rumbling stopped, and Zarina replied. Her voice hardly reached them, even though she was shouting. She spoke for a long time, then stopped and bowed her head.

The giant claw now beckoned towards Amargor, who went forward to stand beside Zarina. Again there was a rumbling question, and a long shouted answer. At the end of his speech, Amargor, like Zarina, stood with bowed head in silence.

The claw withdrew, and the great shape behind the waterfall seemed to draw itself up even higher, as high as a tower, or a lighthouse. It began to turn in the glowing radiance, around and around in a sort of dance, and its great swishing tail broke through the surface of the falling water as it turned. A kind of chant or song rumbled out into the canyon. It was wordless, but the brujos took up the rhythm, softly at first but then louder, singing with a single word.

'Iguando . . . Iguando . . . Iguando . . . ' they sang, beating with their wands on the rock.

From the soaking sky, birds began to descend, perching everywhere on the ledges of the canyon walls. There were boat-billed heron and white-faced ibis, king vultures and double-toothed kites, red-throated caracaras and green shrike-vireos, yellow-cheeked parrots and chachalacas. In the thundering, pounding din of the canyon, their voices could be heard – the '*yoik, yoik, yoik*' of the yellow-cheeked parrots, and the '*cha-ca-lac, cha-ca-lac*' of the chachalacas. And there were other cries too, that Ben and Claire had never heard before.

Then animals started to file into the gorge – tuco-tucos and agoutis, red-backed squirrel monkeys and sloths, armadillos and lizards. And, intermingled with these, were strange animals that Ben and Claire had never seen before. Their snorts and cries and grunts swelled the rhythm of the chanting.

Now the gigantic god of Iguando stopped dancing and thrust a great reptilian hand out towards the rock where Zarina and Amargor stood side by side. Impossibly, amidst all that tumbling water, the hand bore a flame, a ball of fire which burned brightly. The fire grew from thin air, there was no visible burning material – no wood or coals to feed the flames. The fire was set down on the rock and the deep rumbling voice of the god boomed through the air.

Amargor and Zarina bowed deeply, and Amargor gestured to the brujos behind him. Two hurried forward with an iron pot, which he filled with water from the splash pool.

Then birds flew down, one by one, bearing in their beaks a leaf, or a small root, or a clutch of berries. One after another they came, until a pile of fragments lay beside the chief of the brujos. He put a small amount of everything into the pot of water, and then placed the pot in the centre of the fire, which burned brightly with a greenish flame beside him.

Zarina bowed low to the god, and then walked back to the party. Ben trembled. Now they were going to learn their doom!

23
Potion of Dreams

'This is what the god has said. He has been merciful. You are not to die. But you must drink a special potion which Amargor he is making now, and this will take away all memory of what has happened here. You will be going into a deep sleep, and when you are waking up, you will be back at the base camp. You will know nothing of Iguando.'

'But what about Dad, and the others?' Ben said. 'They'll know all about it, won't they?'

'No. Already they are given a much more powerful potion. They will go into a hot fever, and everything that has happened in Iguando will burn away. We must get them back to Tepestloatan soon, where they can be looked after.'

'What about their notebooks and film from their cameras?' Claire said.

'Everything, it has been destructed already. They will remember nothing of their journey. I tell them that the equipment and baggage was lost in a flooded river. Now – come with me.'

They followed Zarina back to the edge of the splash pool, where Amargor stirred the bubbling contents of the iron pot in the middle of the fuel-less fire. He glanced up at them, with a look of undisguised hatred. The great shape behind the waterfall was motionless.

Zarina spoke to the children.

'We cannot give the stronger potion to children – the fever is so strong it could make you die. And this potion, that they are making now, it does not always work completely. It can be that some memory of Iguando may remain with you. For this reason you must face the god, and submit in your minds to keep his secret.'

'What does that mean?' Ben said. 'How must we face him?'

'You will see,' Zarina said. 'Now, you must walk along the edge of the pool to where the water is hitting. There is a gap there. At that place you can come behind the waterfall into the space on the other side.'

'I don't want to go back there. I'm frightened!' Claire said. She could only think of that giant claw, piercing the waterfall.

'Me too!' Ben added.

'You must be brave!' Zarina said. 'This is the only way. The god has chosen what I say over what Amargor says only on this condition. If your courage fails you, then all must die!' She glanced at the malevolent Chief of the brujos, who still stirred his pot.

'Including me,' she added.

Ben felt as if he would dissolve away into water out of pure fear. Claire grasped his hand.

'Come on then,' she said, her whole body shaking, 'now for it!'

Together they edged along the slippery rocks towards the waterfall. Ben felt desperate to turn back, but Claire's resolve strengthened his own. Ahead, the light seemed to dance hypnotically in the cascade, making the tumbling water look like a river of silver and diamonds.

Now they were right there, where the water smashed into the pool. Two more steps would take them through, to whatever lay beyond.

'Ready?' Claire shouted above the deafening roar of the water.

'Ready!' Ben yelled, gripping her hand hard.

'One, two, three!' Claire said, and together they burst into the light.

It was dazzling. Outside, the waterfall dimmed the effect, but here it was so bright that Ben couldn't open his eyes fully. He squinted at the great shape in front of him, shading his eyes with one hand and still hanging on to Claire's hand with the other. All the roar and noise outside only penetrated as a hushed reverberation, as if someone were sweeping leaves inside a cathedral. There was a wonderful smell of fresh vegetation, like cut grass on a summer's day, mixed with hyacinths and roses and jungle. He felt calmed, soothed. His terror subsided into acceptance. Whatever creature was here, it was not evil. It was powerful and awesome, but not wicked.

From out of the brightness ahead, a pair of eyes shone, and a voice both deep and gentle filled the air.

'I speak all languages, and I see all things that

happen, both in and out of Iguando. I see that you are only children, but you love the creatures of the world. You are not destroyers, not burners of forests and killers of hunted creatures. I sense your sympathy. I sense that you have a special love of the living world.'

The voice paused. Ben realised that it had spoken only inside his head, for the voice, once again, was a familiar one. The voice went on, answering his thoughts.

'Yes, Ben, as before in the forest, I take a voice from your memories to speak to you in your own language. I know that you have done what you could, as I asked. But the will of your adult companions has been stronger. Yet understand my message now: you must never lead others to enter Iguando. Iguando is a sacred place. A place important to the earth which nurtures us all. It must remain forever hidden from the greed and destruction that the human race have visited on the green places of the earth. Promise me now that you will honour this trust. Whatever remains in your minds after you have drunk the potion, promise to treat it as no more than a dream, no more than a ghostly image flickering like a poor candle in the bright sunlight of your daily lives. Say now, "I promise".'

'I promise!' Claire said.

'I promise!' Ben said at the same time. He wondered whether Claire was hearing the same voice.

The huge form in the dazzling radiance ahead nodded its vast head.

'I accept your promise,' the deep voice said.

127

Then suddenly the light went out, and nothing but impenetrable darkness lay ahead in the cave behind the waterfall.

Ben and Claire groped their way like two blind mice back out into the canyon. Zarina nodded to them, as if acknowledging their bravery, and motioned them to come forward to receive a mouthful of the potion from a wooden spoon, which she dipped into the steaming pot held by Amargor. The fire had vanished, and so had all the birds and animals that had filled the canyon. Even most of the brujos seemed to have gone, only a handful remaining, standing in a huddle about fifty metres away. The rope with its suspended cages had vanished.

'Where . . . ' Claire began to ask.

'Don't worry!' Zarina said. 'Everyone is safe now. Drink!'

Claire shut her eyes and prepared for something bitter and horrible. But the potion was sweet and fragrant, and she would have liked to drink more of it.

24
The Secret of Iguando

Twenty Years Later...
Claire blinked away the fatigue that pulled at her
eyelids. She was nearly there.

It had been a long drive from Mexico City, but so
different from that long journey all those years ago in a
coffin with a talking corpse, a witch and a parrot. Now
she was piloting herself, in a hired car that moved like a
big cat, with a gentle hiss of cool air-conditioning. The
road too was different – a smooth dual-carriageway. She
kept expecting it to vanish suddenly, to be replaced by a
pot-holed twisting track through thick forest. But it kept
on going – and there was the sign! *Tepestloatan 6k.*
Nearly there.

The town was bigger than she had remembered, and
tall lampposts had sprouted like fast-growing weeds
amongst the old houses. Darkness was falling, but in
Tepestloatan it was kept at bay with a bright electric
glow.

When she found Zarina's house it was in a zone of
new houses on the edge of town. The houses were
arranged around a square, with a children's playground
in the middle of it, and bright green grass being fed by
silvery spurts of water from hidden sprinklers.

Zarina, of course, was older. A handsome woman of about fifty. She had a daughter of twelve. Her husband, an engineer, was away on business. Her English was completely fluent – better than Claire remembered it. Over supper they talked of Claire's time at university, her career in journalism, and her plans for the year of travelling that she was just beginning. Ben and Claire's grandmother had died and left them some money, so Claire was going around the world. A friend was joining her in two days' time in Mexico City, and they would travel on down into South America together.

After Zarina's daughter had gone to bed, they sat out on a small terrace, drinking coffee. Claire brought the conversation around to what was really on her mind, what had been on her mind and in her dreams, on and off, for twenty years.

'Zarina . . . ' she began hesitantly, 'I was hoping to talk to you a little about the expedition.'

Zarina smiled into the night. 'Or non-expedition, you could call it, since you were all struck down with a fever as soon as you got here!'

'Well, it wasn't quite straight away, was it? We did get out into the forest, didn't we?'

'For a couple of days, no more.'

'Well, Ben and I have often talked of what happened, but neither of us can remember those days. And that's strange, isn't it, because we didn't have the fever then, and we *should* remember.'

'You were all very ill. You were kept here in the little

130

hospital run by the church. You were delirious, and your memories were affected.'

'The last thing I can definitely remember is driving with you out to the camp, and finding that everyone had gone.'

'But they came back, you remember? We slept there that night, and they came back. They had just been out in the forest.'

'But then – did we go somewhere else? Ben thinks he can remember a cave. Something strange happening in a cave, with the sound of a waterfall.'

Zarina stood up and switched on a wall light, flooding the little terrace with light. As she sat down again she said, 'No, there was no cave. The expedition had no equipment to go into caves. Perhaps it was one of his dreams – in his fever.'

Claire sipped her coffee for a moment.

'I was thinking,' she resumed, 'that tomorrow, perhaps, I might try to drive to where our camp was. I was hoping it might jog my memory. I have so many strange images in my head from that time, and I don't know if they're memories or dreams. Even this place – Tepestloatan – seems so different from what I thought it was like. I remember – or dreamed – a village of darkness, with flickering torches on the walls. And a dance – surely that was real, a strange dance of people wearing masks?'

Zarina smiled again. 'You are partly right. Tepestloatan was still a forgotten place then, a place of

131

superstitious and old-fashioned ways. The highway had not been built, and most of the houses had no electricity. It was a strange place. But now...'

She gestured to their surroundings. From the bright, modern little terrace they could see other houses with lit-up windows. Inside one of them could be glimpsed the flickering of a television screen, and, in another, a family eating around a kitchen table.

'Now we are part of the modern world. Science has conquered magic, you could say, and we are all in the same boat together!'

Claire took a map out of her bag, and spread it out on the low wooden table between them.

'Could you show me just where we were, on this map. It's the best map I could find, for this area.'

Zarina leaned forward thoughtfully over the map, tracing lines with her slim fingers. She had long red-painted fingernails, and Claire remembered how those hands had once reminded her of a cat's claws.

'Let me see... we drove out along this way. It all used to be virgin forest then...'

'And mountains – there were jagged mountains, weren't there, in the distance?'

'That might have been the Acabo range, to the north. Yes – here is where we went.'

Zarina pointed to an area on the map.

'There is a new road that goes that way. It used to be a dead end, but now you can drive through to Zupacingo. From there you can go on and join the highway to Mexico City without having to come back through Tepestloatan. You will see how things have changed. In only a few years, the modern world has come here, and the old world has gone away.'

Zarina fell silent, and looked out again at the surrounding houses. Claire thought she looked sad. Then Zarina stood up quickly, as if coming to a decision, and said, 'Wait there – I have something for you.'

When Zarina returned, she held out in her palm to Claire a little amulet, threaded onto a loop of very thin leather.

'Thank you!' Claire said, taking it. She examined the gift. The amulet was a small piece of pale green stone, flat, like a piece of slate, and about the size of a tooth. Etched into one side of the stone, in very faint, fine lines, was an image of a lizard's head, like an iguana. From nowhere, a word that sometimes came to Claire in dreams came to her lips.

'Iguando!' she breathed. She looked up at Zarina, who was watching her intently. 'What is *Iguando*?'

For a moment there was a tension in the air between them, a moment full of revelation and unspoken recognition. Then Zarina laughed and smiled, and the moment shattered into little fragments.

'*Iguando?* That is nothing. That is just a word from a dream!'

The next morning, Claire said farewell to Zarina. This would be the last time she would ever see her, she knew.

133

She had been kind and friendly, and Claire was glad she had come. But she had expected something from her, some information or understanding, and she had not provided it.

Claire drove her big whispering cat-like hired car out of Tepestloatan along the route Zarina had indicated. It was not a particularly good road, but it was a lot better than the track of slithery mud that she remembered from before. It had a metalled surface, and at intervals there were little groups of new houses, some only half-built.

After about two hours, she came to the town of Zupacingo. There she filled up the car with petrol at the little petrol station, and bought bread rolls, cheese, and water. On the other side of the town, the road climbed a hill, and at the top Claire pulled off onto the verge. Ahead, in a valley, she could see the main highway back to Mexico City, little shining metallic dots moving quickly along it, like busy ants.

Looking back, she sought in vain for any reminder of the magic of twenty years ago. There were no jagged mountains, no tracts of steaming forest, no tumbling rivers and waterfalls. Just a rather ordinary landscape of little towns and roads, hills and fields, patches of woodland. She wondered if Zarina had sent her the wrong way deliberately. She felt a momentary anger. Was Zarina trying to keep her away from something? Hide something?

She fingered the amulet, which she was wearing around her neck. It was too late now to go back. She had to meet her friend tomorrow, in Mexico City. If there was a secret here at all, then it would have to remain a secret.

Claire reflected for a moment, before driving on. In a way, she felt a sense of relief. It was as if there was a locked drawer in her mind, and she had hoped to find the key for it here. But the key didn't exist. That locked drawer in her mind could guard its secret forever now – the secret of Iguando!

The Midnight Clowns

by Robert Dodds

In the middle of the night, you hear feet on the stairs. They make a sound like wet fish being slapped onto a slab. They must be very big feet. And they're coming closer . . . What would you do if a sinister troupe of supernatural clowns had picked you out as their next victim? That's the terrifying plight that faces Ben Swift and his sister Claire. If they can't find a way to outwit their pursuers, Ben will be forced to drink the clowns' magic blue potion – with terrible consequences!

'A thoroughly spine–chilling thriller, lightened by the realistic and often very funny exchanges.'
Shelf Life, Scottish Book Trust

ISBN 0862649935 £3.99

NIGHTLAND

Robert Dodds

Thirteen-year-old Claire Swift is intrigued by
Aidan, an Irish boy who is new to her school. He
has a secret which he eventually shares with her – at
night, he cycles into another world, one which lies
unsuspected on the fringe of their own. The
Nightland. The Nightland is a beguiling, magical
place but for those who linger in it too long, it
holds deadly danger. One night, Aidan fails to
return from the Nightland. Now Claire, like
Orpheus descending to the underworld to regain
Eurydice, must try to get him back.

**'This book for younger readers should be in
every library for its vocabulary and the
quality of its writing.'** *School Librarian*

ISBN 1842700812 £4.99